INTERNATIONAL BESTSELLING AUTHOR
MARIANNE DAMBRY

ONE SCYTHE FITS ALL

JEEPERS REAPERS: There Goes My Midlife Crisis Series

Somers, New York

This is a work of fiction. Names, characters, places, and incidents are products of the author's imagination or are used fictitiously and are not to be construed as real. Any resemblance to actual events, locations, organizations, or persons, living or dead, is entirely coincidental.

Copyright © 2023 Marianne Dambry

All rights reserved, including the right to reproduce this book or portions of thereof in any form whatsoever without written permission.

ISBN:
First Edition: Coventry Press Ltd. 2023

Cover Design: Glowing Moon Designs
Printed in the USA

For Dad.
I miss you every day to the moon and back.

"Louisa, angels aren't all good, and demons aren't all bad. When it comes to the universe, it's about balance."

Angelica di Mori,
a.k.a. The Angel of Death

Chapter One

"CAN YOU BELIEVE I'M ENGAGED to be married?" I angled my head, ignoring the ghosts peering through my back door. "Falling in love isn't something I expected, let alone thought about at this point in my life."

I had laid down the law. No ghosts in the house when I had company. Not that Thea was company. She practically lived in my kitchen these days, plus, she knew all about my incorporeal charges. Not that she could see them.

"Forty is the new thirty, Louisa. You're seasoned, not sagging. The rest of us should be so lucky."

I turned off the burner just as the teapot's whistle pierced the air, the shrill noise sending the ghosts scattering. I'd have to remember that trick for when my incorporeal guests forgot their manners. Especially around my bedroom and its ensuite bathroom. Not that many have actually been inside the house. That perk was reserved for ghosts with tether issues, and by tether issues I mean problems with the earthly objects to which they had attached themselves.

So far, the weirdest anchor was a Chinese food carton. The white, cardboard kind with the wire handle attached. Turned out he was the type to order food. Eat it. Then complain about the quality and refuse to pay.

I detached him from his foody tether but was glad to hand him over to another Keeper. Service workers toil too damn hard to be abused by creeps, and I didn't trust myself to keep my comments to myself after witnessing what I'm sure were many other incidents to come up in his life audit. Dollars to donuts, he was headed for a long stint in limbo to work on himself.

The ghosts were usually pretty good at respecting my personal space. I was fairly sure my tall, turn-of-the-last-century brownstone with its rooftop garden had something to do with that.

I poured boiling water into two, small ceramic bowls stuffed with Thea's special pick-me-up blend.

"Don't overdo it." She reached toward me with one hand, the bell sleeve on her sheer boho-style shirt slipping to her elbow. The tea is supposed to be thick."

"Thick tea. Yum."

Ignoring me, she slid the porcelain bowls closer to where she sat at the kitchen island. "The trick is all in the wrist." She used a bamboo whisk to whip the contents into a green sludge topped with froth.

"You know, Lou. No one forced you to say yes when Cade asked. If you're having second thoughts, you need to tell him. Though why you'd have second thoughts is beyond me. Cade is everything your ex-husband wasn't."

I looked at her confused. "Who said I was having second thoughts?" A briny scent wafted from the green sludge and my nose wrinkled. "*Gah*! I thought you said this was tea."

"It *is* tea."

"Then why does it smell like fish?"

"It's Japanese koicha. A type of green tea." She continued her speed whisking, her bangle bracelets jingling in time. "As for you having second thoughts, YOU implied that when you were stunned to find a rock on the third finger of your left hand."

"God, no!" I practically sputtered. "Just because I'm stunned to be this happy at this point in my life doesn't mean I'm having second thoughts."

The wrinkle between Thea's arched brows made me nervous. Was I giving off cold feet vibes and didn't know it? What if Cade suspected the same? Thea was witchy and super intuitive. Could there be something to what she sensed?

The thought of not being with Cade for the rest of my life dissolved any false doubt. I loved him. So there was no question about marrying him.

"Thea, stop. I'm pretty happy. Hopeful even. Which you know is uncharacteristic for me, so retract your antennae. Do I flinch a little whenever I say the H-word

One Scythe Fits All

out loud? Sometimes. It's like that old Italian saying about spitting in the air."

"And therein lies the crux of it," she replied. "Deep down, you don't think you deserve to be happy. Which is ridiculous."

She tapped the bamboo whisk on the edge of her tea bowl, and then placed the utensil on a napkin. "Drink this." She pushed the green concoction toward me. "Koicha boosts brain health and clears anxiety, and your aura is shimmering with tension. If you're not having second thoughts about Cade, what is it then?"

"I don't know how to explain it, Thea, but something's off."

"Try."

"Consider my track record. My marriage to Marcus was a flop. I stayed at the library longer than I should've, with a boss who made it his business to make me miserable. I saw creepy shadows everywhere, and then an intricate jewelry box shows up on my front stoop, but instead of something shiny and gorgeous, I got ghosts…and if that wasn't freaky enough, I found myself in the employ of Death Central where I'm dogged by reapers and hot flashes from hell." I exhaled. It was exhausting even in the abridged version.

Thea leaned back on her barstool and eyed me. All that was missing was her chewing on a pen top the same way she did at the library when I rolled my eyes about ghosts in the stacks. Now I know better.

"And that entire list deserves a big, fat razzberry," she said. "That's the past. Without which, may I remind you, you'd have never met Cade. Or been able to do the miraculous things you do for the newly departed. Not to mention stopping a celestial coup and saving a woman from a psychotic break from an unwanted connection to rogue reapers."

Thea never ceased to surprise me with how matter of fact and positive she sounded. Even when we worked at the library together, I was always the cynic, and Thea the dreamer. I loved that about her, even when I thought she was an annoying kook with her spells and potions. Lucky for me I realized quickly her second sight was no joke, and something to be respected.

I didn't have to lie or evade who and what I was with Thea. Not anymore. Not since I first realized my connection to Memento Mori, a.k.a. Death Central and questioned my sanity.

Still, knowing people had my back was an uncomfortable feeling. Mostly because it was me who usually carried the mantle of helping others.

"It wasn't just me who stopped the coup, Thea. That was you, too." I couldn't have done it without her, and she needed to know that.

Thea nodded. "I helped, but it was fate, Louisa. Just like you and Cade are meant to be together. Fate, and a little luck."

Luck was the operative word. Though I would have argued otherwise four months ago when the universe turned my world upside down.

Finding out I'd been selected to guide the newly departed toward their next wild adventure wasn't on my bucket list. Especially since those journeys were more life audit than nostalgia, with reapers circling at every turn to gum up the works.

Reapers were pieces of work, whose close proximity sent my forty-year-old body into hot flashes from hell. That's me. Louisa Jericho. Not-so-mild mannered librarian by day and Keeper twenty-four seven.

No other Keeper had the same burn-baby-burn tell for those sneaky poachers. It's been a macabre dance since I first noticed shadows lurking inside reflective surfaces. It boils down to light and dark vying for newly departed souls. Keepers to guide. Reapers to snatch. Sounds like a barrel full of laughs, right?

Still, I was lucky. Lucky to have been given a trial run to see if I even wanted the job. Lucky to have been assigned Cade to help train me in work that sounded crazy and impossible, but not.

Cade. A hotter than hell Level Five Keeper and love of my now very, very long and perpetually youthful life. Another perk of being a Keeper.

To say it's been steep a learning curve was an understatement. Especially since the universe gifted me another talent. I can wield celestial light. Or more precisely, angel fire, as in light and flame begot from the Sword of God, a.k.a. the Archangel Michael. Whatever they say about me, I'm definitely not a one trick pony.

Surprised at how much better I felt after my impromptu confession, I gave Thea's brew another sniff. "So, Koi Fish tea?"

"KOI-CHA tea," she re-emphasized, opening her laptop. "I brought it for a reason, so drink it. You haven't been yourself for days, and this will help. I added something proprietary to the mix. It'll give your lifeforce a boost. Your aura is looking a little wan."

"See? That's the second time you've mentioned my aura. First its shimmer was off, and now it looks wan. I'm telling you something is up."

Thea rolled her eyes and then took another sip of her sludge. "Nothing is up. You are planning a wedding that has the blessing of both celestial sets."

Her index finger popped toward the ceiling and then the floor, and it was so unexpected I had to laugh.

"Heaven and Hell are a construct, Thea. Yes, there's light and dark, and there's a universal divine, but the operative word is universal."

She snorted, searching for something on her laptop. "A universal divine. Try telling that to some people."

"Let's not go there, please." My nose wrinkled for another reason, and it wasn't the tea.

"Do you want me to do a calming spell for you?"

I smiled at my friend. "Nope. I've got my Koi Fish tea, and later there's a bath with lavender oil and my hottie in the works."

"Again…we should all be so lucky."

Thea busied herself with her laptop, sipping her sludge. She still had her new age shop, but after the coup attempt, Memento Mori hired her as a consultant on the occult. Most of her days were spent with her butt on one of my kitchen barstools. Still, she wasn't wrong.

One Scythe Fits All

"Don't you have training?" Thea asked, with her bejeweled computer glasses perched on the end of her nose. "Promoted from Level One to Level Five Keeper in no time. Pretty slick but well deserved, even if you are behind in rules and guidance."

I shrugged, taking a bag of Cheetos from the pantry before second guessing how they'd taste washed down with Thea's sludge, and opted for cheese and crackers.

"Cade said the Level Ones are calling me the Bug Zapper." I chewed a cracker and a small slice of cheddar.

Both brows hiked up before knotting between Thea's eyes. "And Memento Mori lets them get away with that? The city of New York would be crawling with those reptilian body snatchers if you didn't do what you did. Hells Bells, they chittered like a forest full of cicadas."

"Hence the nickname Bug Zapper."

She shivered. "I bet if you said something to Michael, he'd put an end to it. You melted sixteen reapers like a bucket of water poured over the Wicked Witch of the West, revealing a coup neither the Angel of Death nor The Grim knew about right under their noses. You deserve the recognition."

"Forget Michael. The archangel wasn't too happy about my newfound ability since it taps into his light stash, but as it helped the Angel of Death and The Grim out of a bind, he gave me a pass."

Thea pulled her glasses from her face, letting them hang on the beaded chain around her neck. "I still can't get over the fact Angelica and Morana are sisters. Angie and Rani. Go figure."

"Angie's really the only one who calls her that. Still, the Angel of Death and The Grim Reaper. They are definitely opposite sides of the same coin. Light and Dark." I paused, fidgeting with the tea I wasn't drinking. "I know Morana is busy cleaning up her realm, but I still think something's off. I can feel it."

Thea considered me, and since I'd said things were off more than once, I knew she sent her senses out to test vibrations or whatever it was she did.

"I know things have been quiet of late, but perhaps that's normal considering the take down that happened with Morana's reapers," she encouraged.

I appreciated her vote of confidence, but that didn't quell the knot in my stomach. "Between wedding plans and Level Five training, I didn't notice the progressive slump at Memento Mori. It's strange, Thea. Kind of like the way the air stills before a storm. The soul train chugs out of Death Central without much bother from reapers, and that has a lot of us wondering, including me. Everyone except Angelica."

"Girl, she *is* the CEO of Death Central. Maybe she knows something you don't. I can't imagine Angelica isn't paying attention. Not after the universe assigned her sister a conservatorship for basically ruling her realm in absentia. After all, it was Morana's reapers who went rogue and staged a coup."

I exhaled. "The Grim has no choice. She has a watchdog on her butt making sure she gets her reaper ducks in a row. Something she should've done all along."

"There's something else bothering you," Thea said, eyeing me. "Other than a disturbance in the force."

I smirked at her nod to the Star Wars franchise, especially since she knew I was such a geek. There was no hiding anything from Thea, just like there was no hiding anything from Cade. Not for long, anyway.

"Fine. If you must know, I'm bored." I lifted my hand before she could jump to conclusions. "Not with Cade, so don't go there again. I'm bored as a Keeper. My first couple of months were an action-packed baptism by fire, and now that I'm back and actually *have* fire to wield, things are quiet. Too quiet."

She stretched, cracking her back in her chair before reaching for my stash of snacks. "So, you keep saying. Maybe quiet is a good thing. Maybe it's supposed to be this way, so you have time to train. After all, your new nickname implies the Level Ones aren't thrilled with your leapfrog over those with more seniority. Maybe this quietude is a necessary reset after such a huge shakeup."

My phone rang and I glanced at the screen. I expected it to be Cade, but it was Angelica, a.k.a. the Angel of Death. I showed Thea the screen. "Speak of the devil and she appears."

"Not nice, Lou. Maybe she's just checking in. After all, she agreed to officiate at your wedding." Thea pointed at me. "What other bride-to-be can say that?"

Thea almost never called me Lou, so I knew she did it to rein me in. "We'll see." I swiped right to answer.

"Hey, Angie. What's up?... Wait, now? Why? Okay, okay. What about Cade? Fine. Yes. The midtown office…"

Angelica hung up before I could end the call, and Thea's eyes met mine. "That did not sound good."

"Cade is already on his way to midtown. She wants to see us both. There's been a development."

Thea sat up at that. "What kind of development?"

"Your guess is as good as mine, but if she tells me Cade and I can't get married…that there's some Keeper codicil, I swear…" I lifted a hand and let it drop.

Thea's hands covered mine. "Angelica wouldn't have agreed to officiate at the wedding if there was even a hint of a problem. Memento Mori is HER domain. If anyone would know, it would be her."

"You would think."

Thea was probably right, but still. "Look, I know you've got the shop to check on, but could you stay until I get back? If Cade is called elsewhere, I don't want to be alone, and my gut tells me this will require wine. We can order food. Anything you want."

I pushed the plate of crackers and cheese Thea's way, and then grabbed my coat and my bag. Turning toward the foyer and the vestibule door, my stomach knotted at what Angelica hadn't said. If this was something simple, then why was she so adamant and abrupt?

One Scythe Fits All

Umbrellas up. If my gut was right, it was about to rain celestial shoes.

Chapter Two

I LOOKED FROM ANGELICA TO CADE AND back again. From the look on Cade's face, he was as much in the dark as me.

"So. We're both here as requested. Maybe now you can tell us why we've been summoned." I knew I should've waited for Angelica to speak first, but the knot in my stomach wasn't having it.

Angie's office had been redecorated since our last meeting. Instead of glass, chrome, and leather, she had opted for whitewashed oak and dusky pastels.

The floor to-cciling windows were the same, as was the view of midtown Manhattan. People hurried along the sidewalks, oblivious to the fact Death Central sat front and center on Madison Avenue.

One Scythe Fits All

The sun was bright and Angelica's office warm, despite the shiver along my skin. Suffice it to say, my gooseflesh wasn't from the afternoon's wintery chill.

The city had a dusting of snow, giving the illusion of newness and purity despite the wet, grimy asphalt. Storefront windows were bedecked in seasonal finery, adding to the temporary mystique.

The entire city embraced an air of holiday merriment, which made waiting here for the other shoe to drop more than a little depressing.

Angelica sat behind her desk, and Cade and I stood opposite her, still at a loss. Her face wasn't as emphatic as her tone when she called, nor was she her usual serene indifference.

"I don't understand why you're so quiet. Is this some kind of test?" I was being insubordinate, but by now the CEO of Memento Mori should be familiar with my sass. The same went for my intolerance for all things red tape.

I hated the celestial set's partiality for being cryptic. Angie said there was a development, and if it affected me and Cade then we had a right to know.

Her trademark stilettos clicked a soft staccato on the polished floor. If I didn't know better, I'd think that rhythmic tap-tap-tap telegraphed a bundle of nerves. Was her semi-indifference all bravado? Did the Angel of Death suffer from anxiety like the rest of us? Somehow, the idea of Angie with a churning stomach made me like her even more.

14

"Look," Cade interjected. "Lou and I know there's a good reason you asked us here, and that reason must be important, or you wouldn't have been so insistent when you called."

"Insistent? Try rude," I mumbled.

The staccato tapping stopped. "I'm not rude. I merely impart urgency."

"We're not here to debate the finer points of employee relations. You said there was a development but didn't give any context. If there's an issue with the wedding, just say so." My arms were crossed casually at my chest, but my fingers curled into my sleeves, threatening the fine knit.

The statement seemed to throw Angie for a moment. As if it never occurred that's where my immediate line of thinking would go.

"Of course not," she replied quickly. "Your wedding will hopefully proceed as planned."

I didn't have to open my mouth because Cade picked up on the operative word as well. *Hopefully* proceed. Not definitely.

"Angie…" he began, "if someone has objected to our union over fraternization, why did they wait to say something? Lou and I were away for a month and we've been back just as long."

Her fingers went from templed to flat-palmed on the desk as if annoyed. "I'll say it again. No one has objected to you and Louisa tying the knot. I didn't call you here about the wedding."

My shoulders relaxed to a degree, but if she didn't tell us the problem soon, my fingers would tear holes in my sweater.

"If it's not the wedding, then what?" Cade pressed.

She folded her hands on the desk, and her entire demeanor gave off sent-to-the-principal vibes. "Certain actions have come into question. A complaint has been filed, and there is to be an informal preliminary inquiry to determine matters."

The CEO of Death Central didn't blink, but I did. "I'm sorry, *what*?"

"There's nothing wrong with your hearing, Louisa."

Was she serious? "Forgive me, Angie, but it's hard to believe what you just said. And why does it feel like we're speaking to a District Attorney? What was the complaint, and who was it against?"

She kept her steady, off-putting gaze directed at me.

"Me?" My voice rose an octave in skepticism. "What did I do? When?" I looked between Angelica and Cade. "I haven't done much since we foiled your brother's attempt at overthrowing you and your sister using *her* reapers. Any souls I've brought through audit since have been by the book."

"You killed sixteen plus reapers, Louisa." Her reply was irritatingly matter of fact. "Your actions have been brought into question as to whether or not your behavior was impulsive and subsequently resorted to excessive and unnecessary force."

BOOM.

The other shoe dropping kamikaze-style on cue.

I was stunned speechless, but Cade wasn't. "You have got to be kidding me." He threw his hand up, furious. "If it wasn't for Louisa's resourcefulness, for her instincts in enlisting help from both inside and outside Memento Mori, I'd still be separated from my soul…buried in a half-life with no hope of moving on once my mortal body expired. The same goes for Penny…or have you forgotten the Keeper whose soul was originally taken hostage by YOUR brother?"

Angie closed her eyes for a moment before focusing on us again. "I am on your side in this, Louisa. If I could mitigate these accusations, I would, but I can't. My hands are tied."

"But…"

She put her hand up. "Let me finish. We have to meet with the adjudicator and the prosecution in the morning, so I suggest you go home and think about this together. If you can reach Thea and Rose, it would be in your best interests to go over every step you took with them as well. Every decision made."

I watched the angel's face. Her eyes were weary, and there were subtle dark smudges underneath. I didn't think angels experienced exhaustive stress, but here was proof.

"You went to bat for me already, didn't you?" My question was rhetorical, but she nodded anyway.

I didn't have to ask. I saw the fight that preceded her calling us to her office in her eyes, and I was immediately ashamed for my insolent tone.

Cade wrapped my hand in his and squeezed. "What time do you need us here tomorrow?"

"The preliminary meeting won't be held at Memento Mori. The adjudicator is insisting on neutral ground."

"Neutral as in a public place?" I asked.

She shook her head. "Neutral as in not belonging to the light or the dark. We are to meet in limbo."

My mouth fell open at that.

"Where do you want to meet ahead of the jump?" Cade inquired, and I blinked at him, flabbergasted.

Jump? He wasn't fazed at all with the prospect of leaving the earthly plane for one in between and populated by waiting souls.

"Wait…" I interrupted before Angie could respond. "You said limbo, right? I didn't mishear for real this time."

She seemed slightly amused at my shock, and that irked me a bit, but her nod confirmed the impossible, so my nerves ratcheted up a notch.

"How? According to the Keeper handbook, limbo is for the waiting dead. Not the living." Cade and I may have stopped aging since becoming Keepers, but we were definitely NOT dead.

Angelica considered me. "Do you remember when we first met, and you asked what came after Level Five Keeper? I told you then you wouldn't understand."

Nonplussed, my brows knotted between my eyes. "Of course, I remember, but what has that got to do with us going to limbo?"

Cade answered instead. "When a Keeper surpasses a certain level of knowledge, they are gifted with a rare and coveted ability. They become Drifters. They possess the ability to drift between worlds. To traverse the corporeal and incorporeal. They move easily, with purpose, through the realms of both the dark and the light. Higher level Drifters have the ability to escort Keepers across the veil when necessary."

"Exactly," Angie replied. "And this situation falls into the category of necessary."

The angel stood at that point. "We'll meet here tomorrow at noon. Dress warmly. Limbo is very cold for mortals. Even mortals who have stopped aging."

Cade and I didn't speak as we left Angelica's office. Nor did either of us say a word the entire elevator ride to the lobby. It wasn't until we were out on the sidewalk that he grabbed my hand, and we took off at Keeper light speed.

I didn't know where he transported us, but I knew better than to ask. Anger and frustration radiated off of Cade's body, and my stomach dropped when I sensed a fear shimmering around the edges.

Cade wasn't afraid for himself. He was afraid for me. That told me he had more than an inkling of how this inquest could go.

I needed to know what he thought. What he suspected. If he'd ever witnessed this kind of an exploratory inquest. If he had, and things went south, that would explain his fear. Then again, maybe it was fear of the unknown.

One Scythe Fits All

Lord knows I experienced that emotion enough for the both of us these past months. Cade knew how to be a Keeper. I didn't. Not at the beginning anyway. Still, my gut instinct hadn't failed me yet, and I wasn't about to let it now.

We landed on the porch to Angelica's beach house where we spent our first vacation as a new couple. The jury was still out on us at that point, but my feelings changed very quickly when Cade's soul was kidnapped, and his body imprisoned. What's that old saying? You don't know what you've got 'til it's gone? There's a reason old sayings *become* old sayings. They hit the nail on the head, and that nail went right through my heart.

"Nice, Cade." I pulled my jacket closer against the icy wind off the water. "The adjudicator can add trespassing and breaking and entering to the charges against me."

He fished in his pocket and pulled out a set of keys. "Stop worrying. Angelica gave us an open invitation after our beach weekend was cut short the last time we were here. She told us to revisit everything. This is where it started. This is where we found the box with Penny's soul trapped inside. So, this is where we retrace our steps."

I had left Thea waiting at the brownstone with the ghosts. Rose was now a Level One Keeper, so Cade could find her easily enough, but to bring them both here? I wasn't sure about that.

"Thea's working at the brownstone. I promised we'd order in food when we got back from midtown."

He slipped the key into the lock while I shivered beside him. "Call her and tell her what happened. We're going to need her input, too."

The lock snicked open, and we both rushed inside out of the cold. "Whoever likes the beach in wintertime needs their head examined." I stood at the edge of the living room, rubbing my arms up and down.

My teeth stopped chattering enough for me to take inventory of the house. Except for a few cobwebs and an overall chill, the place was just as we left it.

"Well, speed racer," I said, "I hope Grubhub delivers because I doubt there's anything in the fridge but a box of baking soda."

Pulling the refrigerator door open, I gawped at the fully-stocked shelves, wine and all. Had Angelica rented the place for an Airbnb?

I glanced over my shoulder to question Cade, but before either of us could speculate, the door to one of the bedrooms opened, and Thea walked out wrapped in a voluminous bedspread.

"This place was *not* meant for winter." She sneezed, wiping her nose with a tissue from somewhere inside the bulky blanket. "It's colder than a witch's titty, and I can say that since I'm a witch. I don't think you guys thought this through before whisking us out here."

"When did you...how did you...?" I was too gobsmacked to finish the sentence.

Cade grinned at my discomposure, and I punched his arm. "Hey! No laughing. Not when I may be facing the celestial slammer. I've had enough surprises blindsiding me for one day."

That killed his smirk. "I'm sorry, love. I have no idea how Thea got here."

Thea sneezed again. "Angie brought me here. She called and told me to lock up the brownstone and then wait on the stoop, so I did as she asked. The next thing I knew, whoosh! I was here, freezing. I'm not sure what's going on, but I expect you two to stop bickering long enough to fill me in."

Wiping her nose again, she sniffed. "Cheese and rice! Someone light a fire in that fireplace before we get frostbite."

"On it." Cade squatted in front of the hearth to lay the fire while I grabbed three glasses from the cupboard and a bottle of pinot from the fridge.

"I'm sorry you got sucked into this, Thea," I said, closing the fridge door. "If it's any consolation, we were blindsided, too."

Thea settled herself on the couch, nestling even further into her bedspread cocoon. "I'm assuming this has something to do with the development Angelica mentioned when she called the brownstone earlier, and since you said the words *celestial slammer*, I'm going to need details."

She eyed me, but there was nothing but concern on her face. That and a very red nose. "So?" Thea prompted. "Any reason in particular why we're here, or is it just to prove summer is a state of mind?"

"I hope you're comfy," Cade replied. "We've got a long night ahead of us…"

Chapter Three

THE WIND HOWLED OUTSIDE, rattling the windows like the universe was playing shake the cage. Thea was passed out on the couch, one arm draped over her eyes.

The house had warmed significantly with just the fire. I didn't ask, but I think Cade spun a little Keeper magic to keep it roaring while we deconstructed events leading up to Cade's rescue.

"Should we wake her?" he asked, gesturing toward her soft snores.

Dawn was still hours away, so I shook my head. "Leave her be. She looks comfortable."

We discussed every turn of events. Every clue uncovered. From Penny using the jar of coins on the shelf next to the fireplace in this very room to help us identify her ethereal form, to discovering Rose in the psych ward at River East Hospital, to Thea's divinations about the skeleton key anchoring Penny's souls to this plane, and then helping me piece it all together to find Cade. Nothing that happened constituted a breach of conduct or an unacceptable response. Not when reapers were snatching souls from the living and kidnapping Keeper's for hostage.

The more we talked, the more I realized my connection to the people and spirits around me. Emmie called me a Keeper, and she didn't just mean the job. My connection to the heirloom pendant hanging around my throat and how it channeled angel fire through me proved that point. Whichever way I got to this point in my life, it was predestined.

Part of me hated the idea of lives as preordained. Free will was part of the fabric of my being. Yet here I was, facing what was, for better or worse. I chose to say yes to Angelica when my trial period was over, but the rest? Fate was definitely in the game.

My hand instinctively touched the pendant at my throat, and it tingled beneath my fingertips. It was a part of me now. Not in the sense it was a part of the Keepers who gave up slivers of their souls to create its mosaic. No. A part of me in that it chose me to be its conduit.

The charges against me said excessive force. Impulsive and unnecessary actions. I didn't ask for any of this, nor had I purposely looked to add to my Keeper abilities. I was very happy as a Level One.

One Scythe Fits All

Natural abilities. That phrase followed me like a middle name since I signed on the dotted line at Memento Mori. Inherent talent that thrilled and frightened the powers-that-be when I melded my mind with my deceased charges to pinpoint the reasons they were anchored to this plane. To uncover the meaning behind the objects tethering them here. No one taught me that skill. Yet somehow, I knew.

Cade loaded the dishwasher while I sipped what remained of a problem-sized glass of wine. "I didn't think Thea could cook, but I'm glad I was wrong. That chicken with pasta and artichokes was delicious."

"Why?" I asked. "Because her billowy clothing has a higher chance of catching fire at the stove?"

He put a dishwasher tab in the dispenser and shut the appliance door. "No, because she eats takeout more than anyone else I know."

"Thea thinks better with busy work keeping her on her feet. She used to serve that dish with red sauce. I suggested the lemon butter instead."

With a dishtowel over his shoulder, he topped off my wine before his own. "I always knew you had hidden skills."

"Believe it or not, busy work helps me focus, too. Focus and not dwell." The whole time we were in Angelica's office, anger bubbled beneath the surface. I kept it together for the most part for Cade's sake, and even now, for Thea as well. The truth of it sucked. I didn't deserve this.

"Penny for your thoughts?" he asked, touching my fingers resting on the table. "You're a million miles away."

"I'm not, really." I laced my fingers with his and he stood from his chair, taking me with him.

"Tell me."

"I was thinking about Emmie and George. About the night George passed."

"What about it?"

It was a puzzle piece I thought done and dusted, but now? Something niggled, not adding up. "The night George passed in the hospital a reaper came into his room bold as brass. You had gone to tell the nurses he was gone, and I was by myself. It was the first time I'd encountered a reaper up close and personal."

"And?"

I shook my head, still trying to piece it together. "The reaper in the hospital room was nothing like the reapers I encountered recently. Not the one on the subway trying to snatch a living soul. Not the ones who attacked Rose's psyche, and not the ones at the cave where we found you. Why are they so different?

"The one in George's room was human-looking except for her eyes. She had a second lid when she blinked, and her voice was susurrated like a snake's hiss when she pronounced certain words."

He sat on the edge of the kitchen table with me standing between his knees. "There are different levels of reapers same as there are different levels of Keepers. It's that simple. You were the new kid on the block, and word got around you were like a progeny. I'm not surprised they sent a higher level reaper to check for themselves, maybe freak you out in the process."

"Joke was on them. That's the same night Angelica took me to the portal between our world and limbo. It was then I learned about this…" I lifted the pendant. "If I knew then it had the power to spark a coup, I would've told Angelica to keep it."

"She didn't know its capabilities either. If she did, I doubt she would've let you keep it."

I frowned at that. "She certainly knows now. Why doesn't she take it and hide it somewhere deep in Memento Mori?"

"Because she likes having you as a secret weapon."

Smirking at that, I couldn't help a small snort. "Not so secret anymore." I stepped back, shaking my head because I still couldn't wrap my head around having to face an inquiry.

"What is it?" he asked.

With an exhale, I met his concern. "The reapers broke the pact when they took souls before their time."

"True."

"Has anyone bothered to ask how or why?"

"What do you mean?"

Gesturing fruitlessly, I pace to the fridge and back. "We know Angelica and Morana's brother organized the coup attempt, but we don't know how he managed to do so. Was Yaz that powerful an angel?"

"No," Cade replied. "He was a Watcher Angel with strikes against him for hooking up with the humans he was supposed to look after."

"So, a Watcher Angel is what we call a Guardian Angel?"

"Basically."

I nodded, chewing on my bottom lip. "It makes you wonder where did Yaz, a low-level angel, get the idea for a coup, and how did he manage to coerce squads of lower level reapers to follow him?"

"Well, the reapers you zapped weren't exactly the sharpest tools in The Grim's shed."

I stopped pacing. "I figured, but still. The more I think about it, the more it seems Yaz needed someone on the inside to give him street cred enough to spearhead taking down his sisters." Nodding to myself, I must've looked crazy. "Someone on the inside who had access to real-time information."

"You think someone was working with him?"

I shrugged. "I don't know, but if I were Angelica or Morana, or even the Big Kahuna himself, Michael, I would want to know."

Insinuating myself between his knees again, I reached up to rest my hand on his cheek. "When you were taken, all I focused on was getting you back in one piece. Getting you back whole…body and soul. Afterward, I didn't care what happened to Yaz or even Morana. Celestial justice wasn't my concern."

"I'm sensing a but…"

One Scythe Fits All

I lifted my shoulder again, letting it drop. "Now that we've spent the whole night talking and dissecting everything that happened…" I shook my head. "I don't know."

"Yes, you do. Tell me."

The heat off Cade's body and his close proximity calmed me. It warmed me to my core and gave me courage. I had hutzpah, but he grounded me in real strength enough to trust my intuition without question.

"My gut is telling me the situation with Yaz was too cut and dried. Too neatly wrapped up. There was more to the grassy knoll that day in Texas, Cade."

He raised an eyebrow. "JFK conspiracy theories?"

"No, dummy. It's an analogy, meaning when events are too neatly put to bed, on closer inspection the pieces don't add up."

"What about Occam's Razor?"

My mouth pressed tight, but he put his index finger over my lips. "I'm playing devil's advocate because that's what the other side will do at tomorrow's inquiry. They will say the simplest explanation tends to be the correct one."

He lifted his finger before I could bite it. "Yeah, if you're lazy and don't want to do the work and examine all sides."

"Lou, you can't be a loose cannon tomorrow."

"So, I'm supposed to lie down and let them make me a convenient scapegoat to reset the balance between light and dark just so The Grim can save face?"

"You think Morana is the one who filed the charges against you?"

I crossed my arms at my chest, squeezing the anger from my throat back into my stomach. "Your guess is as good as mine at this point, but whoever it is better sleep with one eye open. I don't deserve this."

"Speaking of sleep…" Cade pried my arms loose, and then kept my hands in his. "Why don't we sleep on this for now. We've covered everything. Prepared as much as we can for whatever questions the other side throws at us. Best we can do is rest and then wake up and eat pancakes."

I smiled at him, marveling again at how he calmed me to my core. "Pancakes. Chocolate chip or banana?"

"How about both?"

Going up on tip toe, I kissed him quickly. "One of the many reasons I keep you around."

"One reason, huh. How about you show me some of the others in private?"

"It'll be my pleasure."

"That's the whole idea."

Swinging me into his arms, I whooped like a teenager as he carried me toward the bedroom, grateful Thea slept like a rock.

Chapter Four

MY NERVES MADE ME regret the second stack of chocolate chip pancakes I devoured before we left the beach house. Cade used Keeper speed to whoosh Thea home, and us to the brownstone. He wanted to head straight to Memento Mori, but there was no way I was facing whatever it was I had to face with bedhead and a slight hangover.

The ghosts greeted me with their noses pushed against the glass panes in my back door. Since the attempted coup, more and more departed flocked to my yard. It was as though the entire ghost population of New York City guessed I had a superpower in my palms, making me their *it* girl to help them move on.

The entire structure of reapers and Keepers had broken down, so it was no wonder I was the one fingers pointed to for blame.

Lower level Keepers were supposed to get to their appointed souls before reapers swooped in to snatch them for the darkness. From there, souls went to Past Life Assessment for processing and audit journey.

If they were tethered to an earthly anchor, souls and their respective binding objects were placed in a ghost box to wait for a Keeper to break their bond. If the tether was complicated, or the soul disoriented, or their human memories lost to time and circumstance, a higher level Keeper…or me…was called in to free them from the challenging and often corrupted anchor.

Except now there were less and less reapers snatching souls before our duties could be completed. The process of corralling the dearly departed had become a lather, rinse, and repeat scenario. The urgency was gone, and with it the process that made Death Central run like clockwork.

Ectoplasm smeared the glass on my back door. Cade and I were the only ones who could see it, but still. Having ghosts set up camp in my garden was funny at first, until disembodied heads popped through doors and windows vying for my attention.

The ghosts were pretty good at respecting my boundaries, but random head popping was a new thing they discovered, and it freaked me out. So much so, I had Thea ward the outside doors and all the windows.

One Scythe Fits All

The ectoplasmic result was like living with a litter of floating puppies slobbering on the outside glass.

"We need to do something about these ghosts, Cade. There's even more now than when I left to meet you in midtown yesterday."

"I know, love." He waved a pair of translucent forms away from the door. "To be honest, I think it's you. I think they sense you can channel angelic light."

"Great. As if hot flashes from hell as a tell for reaper proximity wasn't bad enough, I'm now a human lighthouse for the city's ghost population."

One translucent finger popped through the keyhole in the doorknob.

"Oops." Cade motioned to the bony digit. "Seems Thea may have missed a spot."

"Ugh! It's like living in a damned fishbowl."

He untied the roman shade on the back door, letting the tiered fabric fall to block the spectral outsiders. "Angelica would be pissed I suggested so, but you *can* send them packing, love. If you're not ready to jump back in, then you're not ready."

Had I been doing my job lately? Yes and no. Training, yes. Working on manuals for new recruits, yes. Dealing directly with the souls that sought me for help? Not exactly.

"Let me turn the suggestion around. Would *you* send them away?"

He shrugged, and the silent subtext gave me my answer. "See? Sending them away doesn't feel right to me either."

"Ghosts have no real concept of time, Lou. Decades. Hours. It's all the same to them. If sending them off is unpalatable, you can always threaten the worst offenders. 'Those who don't respect house rules will be banished.' Or something like that."

That was worth a try. Not a blanket threat but directed at whomever got on my last nerve. I moved to the door and spoke loudly. "You heard the man. If you stick another finger or any other body part through any part of this house, you will be expelled from the premises."

The finger disappeared the same way it came, leaving a slow drip of slime creeping its way down the door toward the floor.

"Slime trails aside, the fish have left the bowl," I said with a satisfied nod. "Now let's see how long the standoff lasts."

"You can't blame the ghosts for that. They have unreliable memories, both short and long term." He paused, holding out a hand for me. "Speaking of fishbowls, I think it's time we thought about which one we're going to swim around in permanently."

"Permanently?" I blurted.

He eyed me with a question in his gaze. "You know what I mean, or at least I hope you do."

I tried to play off my show of insecurity with a wink, before walking to where he stood with his rather gorgeous butt against the kitchen island.

"I thought it was time we discussed our options, but I think I'd rather know why the idea of sharing a home with me is such a scary proposition."

"It's not," I answered quickly. "It's the word permanent. I kind of liked the month we spent roaming around Europe. We could do that. After all, have ghosts, will travel."

"I didn't mean permanent as in nailed to the floorboards, but we need a home base," he explained, though his meaning didn't need a road map.

Even leaning against the counter, he was still so much taller than me. Looking up at him now, it was clear he wasn't buying my tap dance.

Still, he didn't press, and I loved him for it. I think Cade knew it was leftover anxiety from my failed marriage to Marcus. I wanted to marry Cade. Then again, I had wanted to marry Marcus. The difference being, I was an older and wiser Wendy, and Cade wasn't a perpetual Peter Pan. Unlike Marcus.

It was one of the reasons I didn't take the position Marcus offered in the university's Rare Books division before my world blew up Keeper style. The other reason was Cade.

"So, what's the proposal, then?" I asked, watching his face.

A half grin tickled the corner of his mouth, and I exhaled my relief. "Nope," he countered. "I already did one proposal, and I still have the grass stain on my knee to prove it. That, and the fact you said yes. Remember?"

Taking my left hand, he lifted my fingers to his lips to kiss them just above my engagement ring.

"How could I forget?" I murmured, my knees going wobbly at the gentle yet intimate gesture.

He guided my hand to his waist, and the feel of his muscled torso made my stomach flip-flop. "So, love. The choice is yours. Where do we live? Here or uptown?"

The brownstone had been in my family for generations. It was the one thing that rooted my life when everything else went crazy. I had no intention of selling, and the idea of becoming a landlord made me break out in hives.

"I propose we live here, then. There is a ton of space, unlike your expensive shoebox. You have potted plants on your fire escape, while here we have a yard as well as a rooftop garden."

A teasing curve touched his lips. "Where you attract the dead like moths to a bug zapper."

"Seriously?" I balked. "You're enjoying that nickname just a little too much."

"Would it help to know they also call you the M-80? Small but powerful."

I rolled my eyes. "Right, because being compared to electric death or a dangerous firecracker is such a compliment. Do you think ghosts loitering in the hallway outside our apartment, and hitching rides with me in the elevator every time I leave or come home is a fun prospect? You deal with ghosts one at a time, and only those placed in your charge.

One Scythe Fits All

"I don't have that luxury anymore. I don't understand why, but at least here, I have the option of ejecting ghosts if necessary. If we move into your apartment, it would be like living inside Disney's Haunted Mansion. A phantasmic free for all. If I'm this tense now, imagine how I'll be then."

He wrapped his arms around me with a chuckle. "I think we should add Pitbull to the nickname list. You had me at yard and rooftop garden, so stop trying to convince me."

The latch rattled on the back door, and we both turned. Obviously, some of the ghosts hadn't gotten the banishment memo.

"What are we going to do about them?" The question was more for me than Cade. Neither of us knew why I had become this spectral beacon, but it was up to me to find out.

The grandfather clock on the landing above the hall chimed nine am, and Cade looked from me to the back door again.

"No, Cade. We don't have time to go killer Keeper," I replied, but it was too late.

He walked me backwards from him, already planning. "We have three hours before we have to meet Angelica and Clarence. If we work together, we can clear a soul or two before we have to leave."

"Clarence?" I asked, moving to grab a carton of orange juice from the refrigerator.

"He's the Drifter who facilitates realm jumps for Memento Mori staff."

I poured two glasses of juice. If I was headed for a mind meld, I'd need the sugar. "Huh. Makes me think of the cute angel from *It's a Wonderful Life*."

Cade's half-grin was very knowing. There was a juicy story behind it, but the door latch rattled again before I could ask, and I slid my eyes sideways. "Ugh. I wish they'd give it a rest. Or GO to their rest."

"Don't let their numbers throw you. One ghost at a time, Lou. The others will wait."

Cade was right, and my stomach went from a bundle of nerves to rock solid again. This was my element. I had done mind melds enough to know what to expect, and if something wonky happened, Cade was with me.

"With all the strangeness happening, I want you to ground me when I go under," I acknowledged. "The last thing I need is to end up with wraith bends."

His brows knotted, confused. "I've never heard of wraith bends."

"Fatigue. Vertigo. Shortness of breath. Ringing in my ears. Not to mention I'm frozen to the marrow the longer I'm under with a soul."

"Wraith bends." He nodded. "Good name. We should make it official."

"Memento Mori can call it whatever they want. Wraith Bends. Spirit Sickness. Mind Meld Malaise. I want to avoid it like the plague today. I need to be sharp, later."

I went to hand him his juice, but he turned for the kitchen door without a word. I heard him rush up the stairs to the second floor, and after a minute or two, he walked back carrying the ghost box Memento Mori assigned me for my test run as a Keeper.

"We can use this to hold the ghosts we clear until we leave for midtown," he said, putting the box on the counter. "I can run them to Past Life Assessment before the jump."

The box's lid had a Keeper sigil that matched the one on Cade's palm. In fact, it matched every other Keepers' mark except mine. After everything, my mark was still inverted. The mirror image of the one on the box and on Cade's hand.

I put my palm over the lid's sigil and the box's lock snicked open. Lifting the top, I took out the music box still inside. It was the one item Memento Mori allowed me to keep. The tether that was linked to Emmie. I missed the eccentric old woman every day I drew breath, and my chest squeezed. She was the reason I was here. The reason I agreed to become a Keeper. The reason I met Cade.

"The music box can stay inside, Lou. It still carries Emmie's essence, so the ghosts will leave it be."

I put it back and then closed the lid without sealing the lock. With a nod, I turned for the back door. "Let's do this."

Chapter Five

HALF EXPECTING A LINE OF GHOSTS to fall into my kitchen domino style the moment I opened the door, I was surprised at how orderly they stood, waiting.

"Wow. Who are you and what have you done with my ghosts?" I asked with a half laugh.

"Maybe they finally learned how to read the room."

I scanned the line of waiting souls. They were unfinished, and as gray as they were translucent, but in each I saw a face and the outline of a body.

My gaze kept returning to a female ghost who looked to be in her early thirties. Her ethereal form shimmered in a short-waisted halter top dress with a full skirt. I was surprised I could tell pinkish polish on her sandaled toes. She wore her hair parted to one side in a sleek page boy style, with a flower pinned up on one side.

She was the picture of a 1950s suburban housewife, except for the large head wound matting her hair above her temple and the corresponding blood smeared on her cheek and down the side of her neck.

"She should be sporting a Jell-O mold, not blunt-force trauma to her head," I whispered.

"I'm guessing tag, she's it?" Cade asked.

I nodded, not sure I wanted to know what happened to the poor woman, but also knowing I had to find out.

Moving to stand in front of her, I steeled myself for whatever emotions were waiting to batter me. "I'm Louisa," I calmly introduced myself, "but I'm guessing you already know that."

She inclined her head, and a few shimmering drops of translucent blood fell toward the grass, disappearing before they hit the ground.

"I'm going to help you, honey. It won't be pleasant, but it will allow you to move on with your journey."

Murmur from the other spirits reached an impatient hum, making the ghost shrink back from me. I wasn't having it. I could only work one at a time, and this was not devolving into the ghost version of I was here first.

My yard was tiny, but this was New York City. I was lucky to have any bit of green at all. Like my rooftop, this was a little patch of paradise, complete with a cement birdbath and two small trees that nearly reached the top edge of the six-foot security fence lining the small garden yard. Grumbling spirits weren't going to ruin it.

"Listen up. The rest of you can either wait your turn by the fence, or you can leave. And no sliming the birdbath. While I'm no Snow White, if you foul the birds' water, I *will* go Huntsman on what's left of you."

I waited for them to file away, their complaining moans mellowing to nothing. I expect they were curious to watch what happened with Miss Housewife 1950.

"You're up, love," Cade flanked my right side. "How do you want me to ground you? You could home in on the sound of my voice, but I'm not sure that's the best anchor. Me talking while you're mid-merge might confuse the connection."

"You need to be linked with me in some way, but not jam my mojo."

"What if I keep my hand on your waist? If you can't hear me, you can focus on my touch."

If he thought talking during the mind-meld would throw me off, then he had no idea what his touch did to my insides. Note to self. Show Cade later. Focus on show, not tell.

Fingers crossed, I gave him a nod and then addressed the ghost. "Can you tell me your name, sweetheart?"

Death robbed each spirit of something, so I had taught myself not to expect anything. Some had vivid recall, while others could barely speak, if at all. Some remembered fragments of their lives, while others had no clue who they were or even that they had even passed on.

She mouthed her name, and a faint whisper tickled my ear. "Charlotte?" I asked to be sure.

Two dimples appeared with a shy smile, and she nodded.

"Can you tell me anything about yourself? Where you lived? How you died?"

One translucent hand lifted to the wound on her head, and silvery tears showed in her eyes. At least she knew she had passed on. Having to convince someone they were no longer among the living wasn't an easy task. The range of emotions went from distrust and disbelief to anger and then some.

Ghosts who didn't know they were dead suffered the five stages of grief in quick succession, and the headache that caused, both physically for me and emotionally for them, was painful in the extreme.

"Can you tell me anything about you that might help pinpoint why you're still here?" I asked, but I didn't hold out much hope. It was clear, the ghost was no longer capable of much speech.

Charlotte opened her hand, showing me a button in her palm. It was gold, with an embossed anchor design like you'd see on a men's jacket. Blue thread clung to the button's shank, and the ghost played with the frayed edges, running her thumb back and forth, sending tiny ripples into the translucence.

"We should get started," I said, and Charlotte did the strangest thing in reply. Turning her palm over, she let the button fall toward the grass.

I expected the ethereal anchor to evaporate the same as her blood droplets, but it didn't. It bounced from the grass to the narrow flagstone path, landing with a soft plink.

"What the—?" I looked at Cade, and he must've read my mind, because he immediately bent for button.

This was unusual to say the least, and in our business, especially of late, anything out of the norm needed to be questioned.

One of Cade's hidden talents was the ability to determine if someone or something was false. Angelica had called him a human lie detector, but it went deeper than that.

While I followed my gut, and could read vibrations before channeling energy, Cade could delve even deeper. He was a celestial bloodhound in that he sensed origin and purpose. He knew the genuine article when he touched it, whether it be a memory or an object.

"Well?" I asked, quickly eyeing the other ghosts.

He nodded. "It's real, and its powerful."

Dropping the button into my palm, he closed my fingers over the small, round item. "It's her anchor. Have at it, love."

Keeping my breath even and calm, my eyelids fluttered and then closed. Ten seconds passed and I disconnected from reality. The weight of the button and its abrupt, unnatural chill were all I knew.

One Scythe Fits All

"Lou, can you sense me?" Cade's voice feathered across my mind.

"Yes. Stay if you want, but you need to let me do this alone. Be quiet."

"Yes, boss."

"Cade."

"Shutting up now."

A familiar crackle started in the center of my palm, radiating outward. Practiced now, I trusted the feeling to go where it needed. Trusted, yes. Liked? No way.

The crackle was pure energy. Like the universe itself coalesced in my palm. Live current spread from my hand up my arm to my throat and into my chest. Crackling fingers constricted as if squeezing blood from my heart while choking the breath from my lungs.

The chill from the button splintered out to my veins as if freezing my blood solid. My throat tightened making it hard to breathe, so I slowed my inhalation and exhaled, tamping down on the sliver of fear that hit me every time. It was the process. The merging of a living mind with a deceased entity.

The crackling heightened to a full-on body buzz and my limbs numbed, the same way my hand went numb when I gripped my vibrator for too long.

I floated in heralded emptiness. I heard nothing. Sensed nothing. Only my own anticipation.

Images formed slowly. Fragmented and jagged. Like always. I saw Charlotte. The perfect hostess. She stood poolside at a summer party, with bunting and holiday decorations adorning a lavish, suburban yard.

The image shifted. Same day, just later that night. A chill drifted past as I watched Charlotte gather empty cocktail glasses on a tray. This chill was different from the earlier cold. This chill was anxious. Defensive.

"C'mon, Charlie girl. Leave that and have a drink with me." A man stood half in shadow by the patio bar cart. *"I've been waiting to get you alone all day."*

She moved the tray in front of her like a shield. "Go home, Stan. Your wife left hours ago."

"Nah, Shirley's fine. I told her I'd stick around and give you a hand."

Charlotte's shoulders tensed, the way prey senses danger before the chase.

"Shirl's a good girl. Too good. If you catch my drift."

Charlotte gave him a nervous smile, maneuvering away from his proximity. "Maybe you should give her a call. She's probably worried."

It was then I noticed a dark shadow at the edge of the yard. It scuttled closer. Like a spider. I swallowed against the lump forming in my throat. That scuttle was too familiar. I'd seen it before, along with the chittering noise that followed.

"Huh. The cicadas are out in number tonight. I'm surprised, considering it's gone chilly." Stan slipped his jacket on, and I knew immediately the button in my hand matched the ones on his cuffs.

"Yep. Chilly," he reiterated. *"Maybe we could start a fire..."* He paused, leaning into the double entendre. *"...and get to know each other better."*

One Scythe Fits All

"I don't think so, Stan. I'm pretty tired. I think you should go home."

He snorted, and then drained his drink. "That's no fun. I thought you were fun, Charlie girl."

"Stop calling me that. That was Daniel's nickname for me, and I don't like the tone you use."

"Apologies to the merry widow." He did a mock bow. "...But methinks Lady Fitzgerald doth protest too much."

Charlotte frowned at him. "You're acting like a cad, Stan. Go home and sleep it off."

An oily feel coated my senses, so I narrowed my focus. A shadowy mist swirled in the perimeter gloom, crawling serpentine-like across the edges. The chittering grew louder, more insistent. It was then I saw the black tendrils curling around Stan's legs and chest.

He wasn't drunk. The man was under compulsion. This was purposeful. Targeted. Like the way reapers targeted Rose and sent her to the psych ward.

"I'm not that drunk."

"I don't care. I said go home. Please don't make me call your wife."

He laughed at that, but any remnant of humor was gone. Even his eyes had changed. They were darker, and his focus had turned almost malevolent.

"My wife, ha! The woman might as well be a nun. Shirley wouldn't get hot if I sat her on the stove."

He moved toward Charlotte. "She doesn't understand need...but you do. Don'tcha, Charlie girl?"

"Stan, you're drunk. I'm giving you thirty seconds to get off my property. If you don't leave, I won't be calling Shirley. I'll call the police."

He put his empty glass down with a bang. "You're a bitch, and a tease. Good ole Danny boy loved to brag how you were his Irish firecracker. How you loved to light his wick 'til he blew like a roman candle." Stan's sneer was as crude as his words.

The situation shifted from troublesome taunt to tangible threat, and Charlotte backed away, glancing over her shoulder toward the living room sliders.

"Danny boy has been gone six months, and a woman like you doesn't just turn it off. Six months with no one to scratch that itch." He licked his lips. "That itch is probably so bad right now, you'd beg for it."

"Don't speak to me like that, you pig! No wonder Shirley wants nothing to do with you."

Charlotte turned for the sliding doors, but Stan lunged for her arm. She answered the near miss with a scream that reverberated up my spine sending my own adrenaline racing.

"Stay away from me!" She flung the empty cocktail glasses at him, the crash sending splintered shards everywhere.

He laughed at her, crunching over the broken glass. "Nice try, Charlie girl, but the smell of your fear only makes my mouth water."

Hands shaking, she gripped the tray's handles white-knuckled. "Go to Hell!" Cocking back, she smacked the heavy wood across his face. His arm took the brunt of the blow, but the edge of the wooden handle caught his nose with an audible crack.

"You bitch!" Blood trickled to his mouth, and he wiped the warm crimson with the back of his hand. "You'll pay for that."

Shock rocketed from disbelief to panic, and a terrified scream ripped from her throat. She turned to run, but Stan caught her arm, twisting it hard.

"Please! Let me go!"

Forcing her to her knees, he s licked the blood from his mouth with a snarl. "See? I told I'd make you beg."

Stan's eyes were black, and I watched helplessly as Charlotte fought him off, desperate for something, anything to free herself.

He tore at her clothes, cursing her and all women. Finding strength from somewhere, her fingers locked around the stone she used to stop the bunting from billowing up. With a savage cry, she bashed the stone across Stan's head.

He fell backward with a crash, and she didn't wait to see if he was alive or dead. She scrambled to her feet, but her foot tangled in the leg of a chaise lounge, and she fell with a scream, smacking her head on the edge of the pool.

She wasn't dead. I felt it. I knew it. So why was she showing me this scene?

Chapter Six

SHE WASN'T DEAD. I was a Keeper, performing a spirit dive into a ghost's last memories, or so I thought.

Concerned, I didn't know what to do. I hadn't encountered anything like this with any other ghost. If these weren't Charlotte's last moments, there had to be a reason this memory and its imprints were shown to me. But why?

Cade didn't offer an explanation. Either he was just as thrown, or he was giving me space to figure it out on my own. I was the Bug Zapper. A Keeper wunderkind, with a hot flash tell and angel fire at the ready. Yeah, because that and $2.75 would get you on a city bus.

Charlotte's anchoring memory was forged before death. That wasn't the irregular part. All anchoring moments were made before death, but as in minutes before, *not* years. It was unheard of, or at least as far as the Keeper texts I'd read.

The answer had to be in what Charlotte showed me, and I wasn't looking closely enough. I focused on the last scene again. Charlotte's unmoving form. Stan crumpled on the concrete. The scene seemed frozen, like a locked computer screen. That is until I heard the chittering again.

Stan's body jerked before going still, and in that moment, the black mist left Stan's body and moved to hover over Charlotte. My entire body tensed. This wasn't just irregular. This was criminal.

The chittering increased from the edge of the grounds, and two reapers crept from the shadows. Disbelief bubbled to my throat. This was not happening. It couldn't be.

Creeping reptile-like across the property, the reapers targeted Charlotte's inert form. Blood puddled under her head, but they ignored the obvious. Instead, they circled her like sharks, assessing.

Chest tight, my breath came short and fast. Every part of my being wanted to rush in and fry the reapers to ash. I had to calm my mind or risk breaking the connection with the ghost.

Inhaling, I counted to ten. In. Out. Having to remind myself to breathe during a spirit dive sounded silly, but when visions were this visceral it was easy to forget.

The scene waited, as if knowing I needed a moment, and I swore the reapers turned their beady, reptilian eyes to mine.

Chittering loudly, they circled one last time before one held Charlotte's shoulders, while the other climbed onto her chest. The creature raised its hand, and my stomach knotted. Were they forming another unnatural bond as they did with Rose?

No. With Rose, they infiltrated her mind with septic bile. This was different. With one stealth move, the reaper pierced clawed fingers through Charlotte's ribs as though slicing through butter. The move was seamless. Practiced. And my gut tightened at the familiarity.

When it pulled its clawed hand back, it held something small in its grasp. Small and jagged edged, like a broken crystal that glimmered blue with flecks of gold.

My heart broke. That black mist and its reapers had fractured Charlotte's soul, taking a piece of her essence.

The woman's body jerked in protest. Whether it was Keeper sense or just what I'd learned on the job, that spasm wasn't just from her trauma. It was her spirit shrinking in response to the stolen piece of her soul.

My palms itched with the need to save this poor woman. To end the reapers and the blackness that caused her pain. There was nothing I could do.

Even if I had the ability to transcend time and space, I didn't have the celestial grace to restore her soul, and frying the reapers responsible wasn't enough. They hadn't acted alone.

The feeling of helplessness nearly brought me to my knees, and Cade tightened his grip on my waist.

"It's okay, love. I got you. Let the helplessness wash through you and then pass. We can't do anything about what was, but we can do something about what is. Focus on the here and now. What we can do for Charlotte to help her find peace and move on."

I had asked him not to intervene, but hearing his voice feather across my mind steadied me. Truth was Cade understood me in more ways than just being a Keeper. He knew me. The real me. My strengths and my weaknesses. What motivated and what annoyed. A fact that both comforted and alarmed me at the same time.

Before I could respond, the scene changed again. First responders cordoned off the pool deck. The police had Stan in custody, and EMTs had Charlotte rushed to the hospital.

Images flickered past like pictures in a photo album. Charlotte in the aftermath. She survived, but she was never the same. The false accusations. The boys will be boys consensus, and Stan's satisfied sneer. Years of depression, alcohol, and pills until she finally took her own life.

The visions dimmed, and the chill receded as did the numbing sensation across my body. My muscles relaxed. I opened my eyes to meet Charlotte's brimming with translucent tears.

"This is not your fault, honey. You are the victim here, and I am so, so sorry."

I hesitated with what I needed to say next. Charlotte was a victim, but Stan was as well. As foul as that fact tasted, it remained clear. Something dark used him to further their ends. Would Charlotte understand he was compelled to do what he did? Would it help?

I looked at Cade. "Did you see any of that through our link?"

"I saw it all, Lou. I also know what you're thinking, and Charlotte doesn't need to know. It won't serve anyone."

I shook my head. "I don't agree. It won't change what happened, but it might lessen the resentment and guilt I know she harbors. I sensed it in her mind, Cade. It's a cancer eating what's left of her spirit."

I turned, only to see confusion on the ethereal woman's face. "It's okay to feel thrown, Charlotte. There was a lot you wouldn't have understood, let alone knew happened."

She nodded, unsure, and I knew I had to do better. "You know Cade and I are Keepers, right?"

She nodded again, this time with shimmery tears wetting her cheeks. No matter how many times I did a spirit dive, it still boggled me that ghosts could cry.

"Then you know reapers are our opposite and equal."

"Yes." Her response was barely audible.

"When I searched your memories and the residual imprints left behind, did you see yourself after you fell?" I needed to make sure she followed where I was headed. "Did you see those creatures crawl from the shadows?"

Unease etched her ethereal face, and I wished I could hold her hand. "It's okay, honey. They can't hurt you anymore," I replied quickly.

Her reaction told me she not only saw them, but sensed what they did to her, as well.

"Those were reapers. They took something from you. Something very important, and that's why you haven't been able to move on. Cade and I will do what we can to find out why this happened and try to remedy it."

I had skirted over the Stan bit, but Charlotte guessed what I didn't say because she held the button out to me in her hand.

"You're right," I nodded. "There's more, but I'm not sure you'll want to hear it."

She pushed the button closer, and her message was clear. She wanted to know.

I didn't know how to tell her without freaking her out more, so I tried another question. "Did you see anything besides the reapers? Maybe a black mist along the ground by Stan's body?"

Her eyes widened slightly, and she nodded.

"Did you see it move from him to hover over you? It's okay if you didn't realize it then. You wouldn't have known, but did you see it when you shared the memory with me?"

Charlotte's eyes went from recollection to alarm, and her translucent gaze flicked between me and Cade. Considering what happened that night, she had every right to be afraid…and not just of Stan.

"Cade and I believe that mist was a dark entity." I said the words quickly, hoping it would terrorize her less. "We don't know how or why, but my guess is the entity attached itself to Stan because it sensed his abusive character. It's clear he harbored ill thoughts and desires about you, and though he may never have acted on them alone, the darkness sensed his inner cruelty and used that to manipulate him. It compelled Stan to act on his worst fantasies."

Charlotte's mouth dropped in disbelief, and she shook her head before mouthing one word. *Why.*

"I wish I knew." I raised my hand, cringing on the inside for making her relive it all. "But I promise Cade and I will find out. In the meantime, keep that button close. It might be a clue."

I turned to relock the ghost box, but then had another thought. "Charlotte, do you know if Stan is still alive?"

She blinked at me.

Her blank look meant no, and I swore silently. If Stan was still alive, there might be a dark signature buried in his mind. A residual trace we could follow.

"Was he a close neighbor?" I tried a different route. "By close, I mean did you live on the same block?"

This time she nodded, and then mouthed the words, "next door neighbor."

It wasn't much, but it was something. "Thank you, honey. We will do the best we can with the information we have."

One Scythe Fits All

The pained look on her face broke my heart. How could I drop a horrific bomb like this and then leave her on her own?

"You know," I began again. "I rarely let ghosts inside the house, but if you're too frightened to stay out in the open, you're welcome to come inside."

Sparing a glance for the other spirits, she flashed an appreciative smile but still shook her head.

"I get it." My nod answered her silent response. "They're like company for you out here."

Her dimples winked with another smile, and she inclined her head before drifting toward the rest of my ghost lineup.

"Cade…" I dragged in a deep breath, exhausted. "Is it okay if we don't do another spirit dive this morning? I don't have the bends, but I'm drained. Just watching what that poor girl endured—" I couldn't finish the sentence.

"You don't have to ask. Of course, it's okay." He slipped his arm around my shoulders. "What would you like to do? If anything? We still have two hours before we have to be uptown. Hot bath? Hot fudge sundae? Whatever you want. Lady's choice."

"I think—" I don't know why, but I glanced over my shoulder to the ghosts and froze midsentence. "Oh. My. God."

"What?" he asked, tracking my line of sight until he saw what I saw.

Every translucent ghost, including Charlotte, had a dark hole at the center of their chest. A claw-sized hole, with a ragged, shadowy trace and the tiniest flicker a slow, shimmering drip.

"Those unholy soul cheating muthas," I huffed.

"You said a mouthful."

Slack-jawed, I needed a minute to think. "I'm nearly speechless. This means Charlotte wasn't a one off."

"This is bad, Lou." Cade's mouth was a slash. "Most of these souls look as though they've been wandering for a while. Based on their clothing alone these spirits seem to range from mid-20th century to now."

"How is that even possible?" I had found my voice, but I was still nonplussed. "How did an entity harvest pieces of souls without tripping Memento Mori's radar?"

"I don't know, but it doesn't bode well."

I expected Cade to reach for his phone to call Angelica, but he didn't. Maybe he wanted to hash out what we knew before calling in the big dogs.

"Do you think this is all of them? I'd hate the idea of dispossessed spirits wandering with no one to help."

Cade shrugged. "Maybe this is the lot of them. Whoever is responsible would've had to keep their activity quiet. Pigs get slaughtered, so they couldn't afford to get greedy."

"What if you're wrong, though, and there are more fractured souls floating around in the ether?"

He exhaled. "We'd have to find them. Incomplete souls are one thing, it's the ones that might still be among the living that worry me more."

"Why?" I was afraid to ask, but I had to know.

One Scythe Fits All

"The Latin word for soul is *Anima*… Life. Breath. Without it a being is bereft of light. Bereft of existence. A person's soul defines them, Lou. Their divine spark."

I managed a quick look at Charlotte. Thankfully she seemed oblivious to this new bombshell, but it made me think. "Charlotte presented in ghost form as a 1950s housewife, but we know she didn't die until she took her life some years later."

"What are you saying?"

My brows crunched. If this was the case, it was too unbelievable to imagine. "What if she presented that way to us because that was the moment part of her soul died? Perhaps it froze her in that defining moment, in that nightmare once she took her own life."

Cade considered what I said. He looked at the spirits milling about the yard still unaware of anything amiss.

"What you're suggesting is unimaginable. It's why I said I worry more about those that lived through the soul fracture. Without an intact soul, a person withers on the inside. They change. Some go dark. Evil even."

I wanted to ask if that explained serial killers, but now was not the time. I cleared my throat and focused on the *how* for the time being. The why would be a whole other story.

"Fracture," I reiterated. "Is that a metaphor, or is that a thing?"

"You've heard the human saying, heart and soul, right?"

Leave it to Cade to answer a question with a question. "Of course. There's even a cheesy song by that name."

"Exactly. We humans love to fuse our beating organs with that particular spark of the divine as though the two were entwined. They're not. Nonetheless, the elysian core of a human's essence isn't hard to locate for a celestial. Light or dark. What's hard is breaking through to a soul's inner light."

"Or its inner darkness," I added. "What's good for the goose and all."

He shook his head. "Not exactly. For decent people the soul is cocooned, protected. Yet at the same time it's everywhere. It's hard to understand."

We headed for the back door and the kitchen with the ghost box, where I went straight for the open bottle of pinot in the fridge. Lord knows I needed it.

"To be honest, it's no harder that wrapping one's head around the holy trinity. That one still boggles."

He grinned at my fallen away Catholicism. "Yeah, that one's a head scratcher even among the angelic set."

"So…" I poured us each a problem-sized glass of wine. "Fracturing the soul to get at the mushy middle is a real thing, then."

"Like cracking open a mother-of-pearl-covered easter egg for the prize inside."

I looked up from pouring the wine. "Mother-of-pearl?"

"The hardest substance on earth to crack, yet shiny iridescent. Like a pure human soul."

One Scythe Fits All

"Wow." Cade never failed to impress. I filed away the metaphor, but something didn't sit right. "Reaper claws are sharp, but can they really pierce a protected soul without dark help?"

He nodded, lifting his glass of wine in salute. "Sharp as always. My guess is yes, and now it falls to us to figure out who and why."

"Whoa." I lifted my hand, palm out. "Us? I get that we're the dynamic duo according to Memento Mori, but this is way above my paygrade. Above YOUR paygrade. This is a job for Michael, as in archangel."

I chewed my lip while tapping a fingernail on my wine glass. "You know what doesn't add up?"

"Take your pick. The whole thing doesn't add up."

I rolled my eyes. "The souls taken recently, during the coup attempt. Those souls were taken whole. Not in pieces. Angelica swore she and Morana returned them to their rightful owners. But this? How are any of us, Angelica included, to track down slivers of souls?"

"I think we need to scour the archives for any reports of something like this happening in the past," he replied. "Penny remembered reapers stealing souls from the *near* dead during the black plague. Maybe this is connected."

He looked at me then, and his face told me there would be no argument. "Not a word of this to anyone, Lou. Not Angelica. No one. With all devious antics flying around, you and I can't trust anyone but each other. We can no longer be sure who is on what side."

"What about Thea?"

He paused a moment, and then nodded. "Thea, then. She can do some of our human-realm research, starting with Stan the creeper, but I will wipe her memories if she can't respect the need for secrecy."

"Got it. Don't like it, but I got it.

His no argument face softened, and he gave me a close-lipped smile. "I don't like it either, love, but we have no choice.

Grabbing my hand, he slow-twirled me before sliding an arm around my waist. "Now, for a really important question. Where would you like that hot fudge?"

Chapter Seven

WITNESSING A SOUL'S LAST MOMENTS to help free them from a tether holding them to our plane was one thing. Charlotte's tether wasn't even a tether. It was the direct result of a premeditated act. Dollars to donuts, it would prove the same for every soul taking up residence in my backyard.

Cade said for me to put everything else out of my mind until we dealt with the adjudicator, and whatever counsel scum the darkness coughed up from their side.

No one had given me the lowdown on what to expect, and after what I witnessed in Charlotte's head this morning, I didn't think to ask.

If it was possible to feel both exhausted and anxious, I was it. Today was like one of those long travel days, where you start in one time zone and end in another. I was in midtown, then the beach, then home for a quick traipse through a ghost's trauma, and now midtown again. It's no wonder I felt a little queasy.

Of course, pancakes, a hot fudge sundae, and an Italian combo from Sal's Place did not help the situation. I'm a stress eater, and today had been one stress after another.

If a realm jump was anything like it sounded, I was in trouble. The last thing I wanted was to open my mouth in defense of my actions and spew all over the adjudicator and his shoes.

"If this preliminary inquest is so important, where is everyone?" The question barely left my mouth when the elevator opened and a geeky guy with horn-rimmed glasses walked toward where we stood waiting.

"Hello, Clarence," Cade nodded. "Good to see you."

The man's hands were in his pockets, and he rocked back and forth on his heels where he stood. He barely acknowledged Cade's greeting, and the awkward vibe radiating from him didn't instill confidence.

"Are you…" he cleared his throat. "Uhm, I mean, is everyone prepped?"

"Prepped?" I whispered, raising an eyebrow at Cade.

The man's cellphone rang, and he quickly excused himself as if saved by the bell. Literally. He walked toward the floor-to-ceiling windows down the hall from Angelica's office.

"Don't mind him," Cade replied in Clarence's direction. "He's just shy. Angels don't need Drifters to enter and exit realms the way Keepers do, so he does a lot of waiting around."

Angelica had still yet to arrive, so maybe this preliminary inquiry wasn't as big a deal as she made it out to be. If it was, wouldn't she be coaching me on what to say and not say?

I laughed at the optimistic notion. This was Angelica di Mori. The one whose favorite past time was throwing me into the deep end and then sitting back with her popcorn to watch me sink or swim.

The reality of that was sobering, and suddenly my queasy shifted into overdrive. I was used to nervous butterflies. Although mine were usually linked to Cade's proximity and how close we were to skin on skin. These winged assassins were a different species altogether. I had no idea what I faced, but my sour gut told me the odds were not stacked in my favor.

Clarence stood off to the side from us, and I swear I caught him picking his nose. Everything about this felt wrong. As if celestial paperwork had been filed incorrectly or a case of mistaken identity.

"What's the matter?" Cade looked at me worriedly.

"Other than Clarence digging for gold in his nose?" I shook my head. "That and the fact he looks like he'd rather choke on his tongue than speak to a girl? What could possibly be wrong?"

"Louisa."

Cade never called me Louisa. It was either Lou, or love, or some other teasing endearment, so he got my attention.

"What do you want me to say? Something about this whole thing smacks of smoke and mirrors."

He questioned me silently, but my answer wasn't so soundless. "Think about it, Cade. At least thirty ghosts from varying eras have shown up in my yard with pieces missing from their souls. Now I stand accused of unnecessary force against reapers. I think this whole thing is a diversion to stop Angelica from realizing what's been happening right under her nose."

"Morana, then?"

I shook my head. "This is too stealth. Too calculated. Morana is smooth and manipulative, but she's also an attention hog. She could never keep this scope of Machiavellian scheme under her hat that long."

"And Yaz?" Cade asked.

Eyeing him, I saw the unwilling smirk at the corner of his mouth. He knew it, too. Yaz was a putz. He could never orchestrate something of this magnitude.

"Yaz was a patsy. A narcissistic yutz someone used for their own purposes. Someone still in the shadows."

"Patsy. I haven't heard that term since the 1920s."

I pulled a face. "Whatever the term, whoever is behind this played on Yaz's insecurities and his jealousy."

"So, Yaz is the Fredo, and whoever is behind this is Herman Roth?" Cade winked, proud of his *Godfather* analogy.

I rolled my eyes so hard I nearly gave myself vertigo. "I should never have made you watch that movie marathon."

One Scythe Fits All

"We're both right. Yaz was the weakest link. Easy pickings for them to use. His sisters are the Angel of Death and The Grim. It's almost cliché how easy it would be to puff him up, dangle power and a piece of the pie in exchange for betraying his family."

"Well, yeah. Basically." I chewed my lip, forcing myself not to pace. "But why? To what purpose? Reapers snatching souls for the darkness is their function. It's why they were created. Stealing whole souls from the living was bad enough, but it fit with stacking their numbers. Stealing pieces of souls? I don't get it."

He ran a knuckle down my cheek, and the simple touch lowered my shoulders out of my ears again. "I don't either, love. That's what you and I are going to find out as soon as we're done playing crime and punishment."

I took his hand in mine and squeezed it for comfort. "Even if I have to do a deep dive on every ghost in the city."

"I think we need to check up on what happened to the full souls the reapers snatched recently."

"Wait, Angelica didn't take care of that?" My voice rose, and Cade spared a look past his shoulder for Clarence.

I lowered my voice but was still insistent. "I know we were away for a month and totally checked out of Death Central dealings, but it's been twice that since the coup attempt."

He put his finger to his lips, moving with me even farther down the hall. "I believe she did, but don't you want to know for sure? What if there were nuances missed?"

His raised eyebrow spoke volumes. Like Cade, I believed Angelica. Trusted her. She had proven to me more than once, the operative word in the title Angel of Death was still *angel*. Yet she had no idea what Yaz was up to. Neither had Morana. It was par for the course. Higher office, less hands on. Less in touch with those under command.

"Clarence." Angie's voice carried down the hall from her office door. "I've been waiting. What's the hold up?"

He hurried past us as though tugged by an invisible cord. Cade's answer was a shrug when I eyed him, before holding out his arm for me to go ahead.

"I'm sorry, Angelica. There was a miscommunication as to where we were meeting. I didn't realize we were to gather in your office."

She stood in her office doorway even more impeccably dressed than ever in a gold, raw silk dress, matched with champagne-colored stilettos with metallic accent leaves around the back of the shoe and twined down the heel. Topping the outfit was a sheer coordinating coat.

I knew the outfit was for intimidation, and she hit the nail on the head since it screamed celestial power. My own outfit wasn't too shabby, either. A belted power suit, cut to perfection in a rich jewel hue that brought out my eyes and the highlights in my curls.

Inclining my head, I flashed her a soft smile. She may have dressed to make a point, but in doing so she also had my back. Angelica di Mori was every inch the Angel of Death and CEO of Memento Mori. In other words, fuck around and find out.

"I don't think there's enough room in your office to accommodate a realm jump, ma'am." Clarence fidgeted with the side of his glasses, clearly trying not to stutter.

Angie closed her office door. "We're not doing the jump from my office. We are doing so from the roof of the building."

Suddenly the word jump took on a much more visceral meaning. Were we actually supposed to jump? As in off the roof suicide style?

I swallowed the apprehension gripping my throat. If this is what it took, then so be it. I was with Cade. We were both Keepers, a.k.a. immortal until we decided to move on.

My hand was fused with Cade's, and he must've felt the adrenaline razor through me. He moved closer so our arms touched, and then gave my fingers a squeeze.

"It's all good, Lou. Just hang on to me. I won't let you go."

My head jerked to look up at him across my shoulder. Every *Dr. Who* episode I had watched, every dramatic Tardis jump, in and out of the space time continuum, raced through my mind complete with consequences if it didn't work to plan.

"Trust me." Cade's soft grin said he read me like a book. "Would I let anything happen to you?"

"Not on purpose," I mumbled back.

He winked, and we followed Clarence to the stairwell and a door marked fire exit. When he opened the door, I expected a typical set of concrete stairs leading to the roof, but instead there was a metal circular staircase. Much narrower and incredibly steep.

Hmmm. I looked up at the winding steps. "A metal stairway to Heaven. Led Zeppelin would be shocked."

For all I knew, this staircase wasn't visible to average humans, and it was most likely warded against trespassers and demons. Not that demons could pass the threshold at Memento Mori. Or I hoped not.

"Ladies first," Clarence said, pushing his glasses higher on his nose.

Angelica gave him an imperious look. "You are in charge of this jump, Clarence. YOU go first."

The geeky man paled considerably but did as she asked. Clarence first, then Angie, me, and finally Cade. It was go time.

Chapter Eight

"IF YOU MADE CLARENCE GO FIRST because he might peek up your skirt, I'm telling you the man would probably pee himself." I couldn't resist, so I leaned in with a whisper.

Angie didn't reply, but I saw the half smirk at the corner of her mouth. She'd thought it, too.

No one said a word as we climbed. Just metallic footfalls puncturing the quiet. I clenched my teeth against the disjointed clanging. It seemed to grow louder in my head the higher we went on the stairwell's spiral.

It was almost as unnerving as what I faced once we got to the top. Unnerving as in crossing dimensions in time and space, and in facing an inquiry where I had no clue as to my accuser, or for what and why I was being accused. Both grated my spiking anxiety, so I did what I always do. I talked to myself.

"And what are you doing today, Louisa? Funny you should ask. I plan on jumping off the roof of an office building in the heart of midtown, while aiming for a tiny cup on the sidewalk below."

I posed the question and its answer aloud, directed at no one and everyone. When I heard Cade snicker behind me, I kept it up.

"It's a celestial party trick, or so they tell me. Apparently, we'll all disappear into the sidewalk cup, and end up in an alternate reality. An alternate reality you say? Are you sure you don't mean death splat?"

Clarence looked past his shoulder at me, horrified, before sparing a glance for Angelica, but I continued.

"Funny you should suggest *death*, considering the office hosting this jumperific spectacular is actually Death Central."

Angelica paused scaling the stairs for half a second, her stilettos hanging like six inch nails off the edge of each step like a threat. "That's not funny, Louisa."

"Actually, I thought it was pretty clever," Cade chimed in. "In any other circumstance, Lou would be right."

Cade got it, and me. If no one was going to talk about the how, what, and why, then hey, my solo act would continue.

"I suppose my next burning question is what about limbo? I know it's a celestial in between, but what does that look like for individual souls? Does it follow a specific dogma, or is it like the saying, 'Heaven is what you make it?'"

Not a peep other than feet on stairs, and my question wasn't glib. It was a legit ask.

"If it was up to me, limbo would be a giant library with cozy chairs, where everyone had a comfort animal and there'd be an all you can eat café." I waited, but no one corrected me, so I kept going. "As for Heaven, I'd choose a lake house with mountain views and all the amenities, and everlasting batteries for all my adult toys."

Cade coughed out a laugh. "I'll try not to take my battery-operated competition personally."

"Oh, it's *completely* personal," I said, matching his chuckle. "Especially since I know you LOVE a really good…*view*." After my intentional pause, I didn't have to look to see Cade's grin.

"Comedians." Angelica muttered. "Are you two quite finished?"

"Aw, you love us," I teased, glad to know she was still listening.

She snorted. "That's half the problem."

The quiet climb resumed, and by the time we reached the top, my thigh muscles were burning.

"There is no way this spiral deathtrap is up to fire code." I held the metal rail, catching my breath. "It's too high, too narrow, and it takes too damn long to reach the roof."

"It's not up to code," Angie replied, "because it doesn't have to be. No human will ever see this stairway let alone use it."

"If that's the case, why didn't we use Keeper speed to whoosh to the roof? Or is this early penance ahead of whatever reprimand awaits?"

"Louisa, I know your snarky humor is a defense mechanism, but it has to end here. You need to take this seriously." All vestiges of amusement had left Angelica's face, instead there was a flicker of worry that spiked my own even more.

She paused, giving Clarence leave to open the door to the roof. "Look, I don't know who called for this inquest, but it's not something any of us should take lightly. There's a lot that rides on today's outcome, and not just for you."

Angie's expression was all business, so I wiped the nervous kidding from my face. Today was one of those days where I swore the universe reveled in curve balls with my name stitched into the cowhide. Then again, why would the universe zero in on me for anything? It's not like I was part of some master plan, even if it felt that way sometimes.

Clarence put his palm on the roof door, whispering words in the same ancient language I'd heard Angie use in the past. Any other time, I'd focus on the magic in front of my face. Today was not any other day.

"Angelica, you haven't told me much about what I'm facing, and to be honest, that's making me very nervous. Is this to be an informal fact finding mission or more like a deposition?"

Cade covered my hand on the railing while Clarence finished unlocking the ward. "More like mission impossible."

"It's neither," Angelica replied, shooting Cade a look. "As a level five, I expected more backup from *you*."

"Louisa is a level five, as well. Or have you and the others of your celestial set forgotten that detail?" Cade was never deliberately insubordinate. That was usually my thing, but here he was being impertinent on my behalf.

Angelica's eyebrow hiked, and it was clear his nerve wasn't appreciated. I needed to redirect her annoyance back to me, or my problems would become Cade's, and I didn't want that. The vows we planned included in sickness and in health, not in self-will and recklessness. One of us had to embody cooler heads prevail, and I needed that person to be Cade.

"It's okay, babe. I appreciate the support, but fighting amongst ourselves won't help anyone, least of all me."

Angelica nodded. "Thank you, Louisa. I couldn't have said it better myself."

Clarence opened the door, and I followed Angie onto the roof with Cade at my side. "Yeah, but the problem inherent with *that* is you haven't said anything." The CEO of Death Central was used to my sass, so I went for it. "Telling me this inquest is neither informal, nor a deposition isn't an answer, Angelica. It's an evasion and an insult."

"Lou's got a point, Angie. And it's not like I can fill in the blanks, either. In my century and a half as a Keeper, I've never heard of this kind of inquiry. It's not only unusual, it's suspicious."

It was now or never, and I was done dancing around the topic. I'd had enough of the cryptic. This went beyond Angie's usual tightlipped only-when-you-need-to-know drill.

"Why won't you tell me what to expect? You know how I am, Angelica. I'm going to assume the worst until I'm told otherwise, so give me a heads up or I won't be able to keep my cool once we get there!"

"Louisa! I can't!" Angelica threw her arm up, losing her prized control. "Don't you think I would tell you if I could? This entire situation is unprecedented! To have one of *my* Keepers questioned and ME under a gag order?" Her perfectly lined lips trembled in a slash, and the sound that left her throat was frightening.

"This inquiry is a slap in the face and a direct commentary on my leadership. When I find out who filed this level of complaint, I swear…"

She didn't finish the whispered threat. Instead, the sky darkened to ink, and the wind whipped across the city in a sudden tempest. The Angel of Death was pissed.

I pulled my jacket tighter against the violent gusts. "Okay! I get it. Can we save the vengeful goddess thing for the opposition?"

One Scythe Fits All

Her lips pushed to one side in a satisfied smirk and the wind calmed as quickly as it raged, clearing the sky.

Nervy or not, Angelica had a soft spot for my sass. Perhaps allowing me leeway she didn't allow herself was a relief valve of sorts. After seeing this display? I was grateful for cool and collected. The Angel of Death's flip side was scary as hell.

"Thank you," I said, watching Angie smooth her hair as though she didn't send midtown into a cosmic frenzy a' la *Ghostbusters*.

Cade whistled low. "Don't mess with the lady in the stiletto pumps."

"Everyone…" Clarence coughed to get our attention, pretending he didn't just shake in his shoes like the rest of us. "I need you to take your places on the ledge. I've marked each spot accordingly."

My gaze yanked from Cade to the ledge overlooking Madison Avenue. There on the concrete lip were four red x-marks.

"You can't be serious." I shook my head, not needing a mirror to see the knot of disbelief on my face.

I looked at Clarence again, expecting him to yell, *Gotcha!* but he simply lifted an arm out to the roof ledge. "It's all as it should be. Everything is in place."

"For what? A firing squad?" I waved my hands in front of my chest. All my earlier bravado vanished with each backward step I took. *If this is what it took, then so be it. I was with Cade. We were both Keepers, a.k.a. immortal until we decided to move on.* "Nope. No way."

"I thought you were joking when you said jump. I figured that was a metaphor for portal, or doorway. Something that didn't require shouting *Geronimo!*"

"Calm down, Louisa." Angelica followed me as I backed up toward the roof door. "This is very routine."

She looked at Cade for help and then Clarence, who to my surprise, stepped up to the plate.

"Angelica is right, Ms. Jericho. You are perfectly safe," he reassured. "This is my only job. I assure you I know what I'm doing. There's no reason to be nervous. Realm jumping is a piece of angel cake."

The man held out his hand to take mine, and he seemed to grow in stature. His back straightened and his shoulders squared, giving an air of confidence I hadn't seen. Clarence still looked like he spent more time than not playing *Dungeons and Dragons*, but now he exuded mastery. Realms were his element. Like in D&D.

I felt bad about poking fun about him peeing himself. After all, it took a geek to appreciate a geek, even if my geekdom was *Star Wars*. Still, I did catch him picking his nose, so there was no way I was taking his hand.

"Okay. I suppose I have no choice. If Angelica trusts you and your set up, then so do I." I reached for Cade, and Clarence took the hint and dropped his hand.

"Over the top?" Cade asked, squeezing my fingers.

"Until death do we drop."

Angelica rolled her eyes. "Will you two stop with that?"

One Scythe Fits All

Cade and I watched her walk to the ledge where she climbed onto the concrete lip in her stilettos.

"Wow," I murmured. "Fierce."

"Yep," he concurred. "That's why we love her."

The Drifter took his position on the ledge between me and Cade, and then held his hands out to both of us.

"Uhm, I'm good with Cade's hand. Thanks anyway."

"You don't have a choice. You *both* have to take hold of my hands, or your earlier jest will come to pass. Splat on Madison Avenue."

I had hand sanitizer in my pocket, so I slipped my hand into Clarence's waiting palm. Cade did the same, giving me a quick wink.

"Catch you on the flipside, love."

I nodded, holding my breath.

"On the count of three, ready?" The question was rhetorical, and Clarence gripped my hand so tightly I thought I heard my bones snap. "Whatever you do, don't let go."

I had visions of me spinning off into a chasm or landing in the middle of the ocean with no land in sight.

I suddenly couldn't care less about Clarence's cooties. "Don't look down, Louisa. DON'T. LOOK. DOWN."

"Do you often natter to yourself?" Clarence asked.

"Shut up."

"It's okay to peek," he replied, unfazed. "I promise. Nothing untoward is going to happen."

"He's right, love." Cade assured from the other side of our trio. "It's actually quite pretty."

I allowed myself a tiny peek. Cade was right. Everything shimmered, obscuring the street and the traffic below. It was a portal. Just not the kind I expected.

"Oh crap!" I crouched forward involuntarily, as though a strange tether attached itself to my belly. "What the hell is that?"

"It's perfectly normal," the Drifter replied quickly. "Don't panic."

Current sizzled along my skin, making the hairs on my neck and arms stand on end even under my clothes. My body went taut, and something locked inside me, pulling me toward the very precipice.

"I'm going to fall!" A scream formed in my throat. I had no control, as if a tractor beam had locked onto my core.

Wind howled in my ears as if Angelica's maelstrom was back. "Let go, Louisa." The angel's voice feathered across my mind. "Stop fighting it and jump."

Across my shoulder I saw Angelica spread her arms and then jackknife off the edge into the swirling shimmer below.

"Now!"

Clarence jumped, taking Cade and I with him. We hurtled over the edge, and the waiting scream ripped from my lungs.

One Scythe Fits All

The vortex swirled, forcing us into a huddle with the Drifter who seemed to grow in size and strength.

From the sizzle along my skin, I expected extreme heat or a cold so bitter it burned. Instead, the vortex was warm. Like being wrapped in a comfy blanket while still in the dryer.

I squeezed my eyes closed against the force of tumbling, surprised I hadn't tossed my cookies. To stop myself from flailing, I held onto both men white-knuckled. At one point I thought I heard the Drifter whimper. I yelled an apology, but my words were lost to the vortex.

We landed on a flat plateau at the top of a grassy slope. Disoriented, it took a minute for me to let go of our group hug. When I finally opened my eyes, Cade was there with a steadying hand and a quick kiss.

"You okay, killer?" he whispered, but all I could manage was a nod and a lopsided smile.

"Welcome to limbo, kiddos." From the look on Angelica's face, it was clear the celestial spin cycle hadn't fazed her at all. In fact, she looked utterly serene.

Clarence was nowhere to be found, though I suspected he'd materialize when we were ready to return to the earthly plane. Or so I hoped.

Once I found my feet, the first thing I noticed was the large concrete and marble building ahead. It looked unexpectedly like Memento Mori's midtown headquarters. Except there was no city scaffolding and the building itself was pristine. That, and the fact it was perched on a rise above a rolling green vista.

The gargoyles were still at their posts along the top façade, and they turned in acknowledgment. Angelica inclined her head in answering deference before smoothing her dress and her hair.

Still a little shaken, I took inventory of myself as well. Hair? Check. Clothes and shoes? Check. Mind? The jury was still out on that.

"Wow. Death Central looks amazing with no scaffolding and no pigeon poop." Cade gave the gargoyles a thumbs up. "I guess it's easier for our beasties to keep things up-to-snuff in the afterlife."

Nonplussed, I gave the ugly guardians a closer look. "I thought you told me gargoyles were the sentinels against harm."

"Harm comes in many forms, Lou. Have you ever tried cleaning pigeon poop off a windshield? It adheres on a molecular level, and New York pigeons are prolific. Besides, pigeon is a gargoyle favorite. They say it tastes like chicken."

It felt good to laugh, and I slipped my arm into the crook of his elbow. "Don't get any ideas. Flying rats will not make the wedding menu."

"Hey, don't knock it 'til you try it. Pigeon is a delicacy in France."

"Ew. Nope."

Angie grinned at us. "Pigeon poop and gargoyle favorites aside, this is Memento Mori in its purest form. The celestial home to departed souls in wait. Everything around you was created to feel familiar. It was done so by design for souls relegated here for the duration.

One Scythe Fits All

I took in the view from where we stood on the grassy rise. A body of water shimmered in the distance, with soft whitecaps cresting beneath a bridge spanning two shores of sublime coastline.

A quad of cabled spires flanked either side of the bridge's center. Their dizzying height reminded me of a scene from the movie *City of Angels*. Particularly, the fall from grace.

The movie as a whole sucked, with its writers needing a swift kick and a crash course in happily ever after, but knowing what I do now about angels, someone was in the know when they wrote that fall.

"Whoa." I grabbed Cade's arm to get his attention, and I stood slack-jawed with him staring at Angelica.

She faced the water with her arms outstretched, and her face tilted toward the light. Mesmerized, I watched her human guise drop and her angelic form shine with pure abandon. This was no luminous silhouette I had been privy to a few times. No. This was pure angel.

Her wings spread, glorious in scope and shimmering color, and her body glowed with a sheer incandescence that enveloped her whole being.

Angelica was home. There was no other explanation. I watched in awe until Angie's arms lowered to her sides again. Her shoulders rose with a deep inhale, and she turned.

"It's time," she said, sparing a glance toward the building's revolving doors before zeroing in on me. "Whatever you do, Louisa, and with every answer you give, promise me you'll keep your cool."

How could I promise anything when I had no idea what I faced? My gut was already twisting, and not from what I ate, but I nodded anyway. Be professional. Never let them see you sweat. Considering my history since becoming a Keeper? Definitely easier said than done.

Chapter Nine

I STOOD JUST INSIDE THE revolving doors, speechless. Considering the outer façade, I expected a replica of Death Central on the inside as well. What I got was more Department of Motor Vehicles than Memento Mori.

There was no lobby. Just a vast room with rows and rows of benches cordoned into organized groups where the dead awaited processing. A line of souls queued to be called to an array of bank teller-like windows designated by time zone and geographic region.

A feeling of tedium and futility permeated the sterile space, but it was the sense of resignation that got me the most. My upbringing and the dogma taught never painted limbo as a place of comfort, but this was unsettling. The place was devoid of life. Devoid of warmth. And sadly, it seemed devoid of hope.

"So much for a library with comfy chairs and comfort animals," I muttered under my breath.

The desolation was palpable, and I chewed my lip, uneasy, until a realization jerked my gaze to Angelica. "Is this where Emmie would have been sent if I hadn't accepted my role as Keeper?"

"Limbo is for souls in wait, Louisa. Souls whose journeys have been delayed, for whatever reason. Paradise and the comforts therein are the reward at the end of that long wait."

Basically, her canned answer told me I was right. Emmie would've spent eternity sitting on a bench, waiting. Ironic, considering she made her home in a city park before she died, but at least the benches there were surrounded by life and love. Not to mention color.

"This kind of waiting is unacceptable, Angie. Especially when we have a surplus of Keepers with time to kill since the coup attempt." I had to say something. "Maybe they could be reassigned to help move things along here."

Her violet eyes were on me at this point. "Time spent in limbo isn't just about Keeper scarcity. Souls are sometimes sent here while their life audits are reviewed. Sometimes there are questions, or extenuating circumstances that need further investigation before the soul can move on."

"Like when the departed are missing a piece of their souls?" I don't know why I threw that out there, especially when I promised I'd keep our suspicions about what I witnessed in my spirit dive into Charlotte's mind between Cade and myself.

Angelica's expression turned surprised. "Why would you say something like that? I can only assume you're referring to the souls snatched before their time during the coup attempt. I already told you. They were restored."

I had to shift gears and pull both feet out of my mouth before Angie got too suspicious. Investigating what happened to Charlotte and the other ghosts haunting my yard was on the agenda after we got through with this preliminary inquest, and irking the Angel of Death was not the way to get to the bottom of anything.

"What if those souls were damaged after Yaz's antics?" I asked, hoping my turnabout worked.

She waved my concern away, telling me she bought my tap dance. "Stop worrying, Louisa. We have enough on our plate this afternoon without adding to it, and for my sake, do not bring up the possibility of damaged souls during deliberations. We don't need to give the other side any more help."

More help? Was that a Freudian slip? Had Angelica been loose lipped after the coup attempt? Had Morana?

Weighing the odds, The Grim was a more likely candidate considering the size of her ego, and that she now had a watchdog monitoring her every move, and it wasn't a hell hound.

"Ms. di Mori?" A pretty, cherub-looking angel with hair the same reddish color as mine interrupted. "The panel is waiting for you in the main conference room."

Panel? Maybe my original firing squad analogy wasn't as far off as I was led to believe.

The redheaded angel pointed us toward a door off the end of an array of service windows. Angelica led, and we followed like ducks in a row down a white polished corridor also devoid of warmth, until we came to a set of closed double doors. With a wave of her hand, the doors opened in a not so subtle announcement.

"Still making grand entrances, Angelica?" A man in a brown suit with dull yellow pinstriping chuckled from his seat at the end of a long conference table.

A side grin graced Angie's lips as Cade and I filed in behind her. "And deprive you of thinking you know me so well, Enoch? Never."

"I'm glad to see the human world hasn't changed you much," the man teased, pointing a mechanical pencil her way. "Though I do sense a higher level of empathy in you than the last time we saw each other."

An affectionate smirk tugged at her pretty mouth. "What can I say? I'm an old softy."

"Old is relative, and you are never soft." He chuckled again, matching her level of warmth. "At least not at first glance."

She winked at that, and I wasn't sure if it was playfulness between old friends or a slight flirtation. Either way, was that a good omen or a strike against?

One Scythe Fits All

The only other person in the room was a statuesque woman as tall and commanding as Angelica, but without the same incandescent glow. Could angels turn their celestial shimmer on and off? I had never thought to ask and now wasn't the time.

The tall woman's dark hair was styled in a messy pixie cut, revealing slightly pointed ears that gave her a queen of the fairies vibe. She wore a business suit in a cool shade of green, with an official gold-colored stole that reminded me of my college graduation.

"Reggie." Angelica inclined her head, and the affable grin she held for Enoch slimmed to a cool, close-lipped smile. "Why am I not surprised to find you presiding today?"

"Is that any way to show appreciation?" the woman asked with a tsk. "You should be glad I'm overseeing today's proceedings. I have no patience for games. Especially ones spawned in the dark. I heard about your brother and what he tried to pull. It's part of the reason I asked to head this preliminary inquest, and possibly represent your Keeper. I want to cut through the proverbial posturing to zero in on what really happened."

The woman's eyes found me, and I squared my shoulders. Cade's pinky touched my hand, and I exhaled the breath I'd been holding.

"Louisa…" Angelica gestured toward where the man in the brown suit sat at the table. "Let me introduce Enoch Wilder. He's an old friend, and one of our most trusted scribes. Think of his position like a celestial court reporter."

"It's nice to meet you." I gave the man a polite nod, but it wasn't the scribe who interested me. It was the tall pixie who clearly held my fate in this debacle.

"And this regal lady is Raguel, a.k.a. the Archangel of Judgment," Angie continued. "More affectionately known to her friends as Reggie. She will be your adjudicator."

Reggie's assessing gaze made me glad I made an effort with my appearance this morning. One pass of her green eyes told me the woman saw everything. Every flaw. Every poor choice I made during my forty years on earth.

The soft set to her full lips told me she also saw the burden of responsibility I put on myself. The love. The loyalty. The hard work. I knew then she'd be fair, and my shoulders relaxed a notch.

"Ms. Jericho, I'm sure you have as many questions for me as I have for you," Reggie said as if responding to my thoughts. "We'll get to them, I promise. I also promise I will brook no shenanigans from the other side." She frowned glancing at her watch, and for a second she looked like a dark elf. "That's if they deign to show up at all."

No sooner had the words left the adjudicator's mouth than a familiar yet unwelcome sensation stirred in my gut.

One Scythe Fits All

Heat flushed my face, radiating down my throat to my chest where my heart pummeled my ribs like a prison break. I groaned. Not now. Please, not now.

Deep breaths steadied my racing pulse, but it did nothing for the sweat trickling between my breasts. Moisture formed on my forehead, and the bridge of my nose and upper lip. I wiped it away, hoping no one noticed.

The last thing I needed was Reggie to assume perspiration confirmed a guilty conscience. There was only one reason I'd sweat like a spent athlete in high summer. Reapers. Although how they'd found their way into limbo was beyond me.

Hackles up, I stared at the door on the opposite side of the conference room.

"Lou? Are you okay?"

I ignored Cade to concentrate on my breathing.

Any second now.

"Louisa?" Cade's concern had grabbed Angelica as well. "What's wrong?"

I wiped my face again, shivering despite the radiating heat.

Five. Four. Three. Two. One.

BINGO.

The far door opened with a bang, and a tall, lanky man in a black suit, black shirt, and black tie walked in as though he owned the place.

"Apologies for my lateness." He inclined his head to Raguel, ignoring both Enoch and Angelica. Not a good sign. "I'd blame traffic, but as this is limbo…" The sound of his voice twisted my innards, even as he chuckled at his own joke.

"Kushiel, your capacity to inspire both annoyance and ennui astounds me," Reggie wasn't having it. "Take a seat and shut up."

His cheesy, used car salesman grin paled, and he did as the adjudicator requested. "I am sorry for the delay. It was unavoidable."

I stifled a wince, gripping my shirt so I could use my fist as counterpressure against the shards piercing my gut. In all the times reapers set my insides to hot flash inferno, I never experienced pain. Perspiration? Yes. Pain? Never.

"Lou?" Cade whispered my name again. This time more than concern edged his tone.

Angelica caught my wince as well. She placed her hand on my shoulder, and the moment her fingers made contact the pain evaporated. The feverish feel. The sweating. Everything. Gone.

She kept her hand on my shoulder but shot the mother of all death looks across the room. The newcomer winced, his hand going to his temple.

"Arrgh! Objection!" he ground out. "We've yet to begin and hostilities are already in force!"

Angelica narrowed her eyes and this time the man whimpered. "Enduring a tedious and unnecessary inquiry is one thing. I and my team do so in good faith, so I *will not* stand by and let one of mine suffer an underhanded and stealth attack."

"Lies!" His face was red, grunting out the denial.

One Scythe Fits All

"Cut the crap, Kushiel," Angelica shot back. "Your deception stinks worse than my sister after a sulfur bath. You came through that door with silent weapons pointed at my Keeper!"

Reggie raised a questioning brow. "Are you accusing Kush of attacking your Keeper?"

"I'm not accusing. I know! He's in covert reaper mode, knowing full well my Keeper has a unique tell that causes extreme discomfort."

One look at my pained state sent the adjudicator's frown rocketing from doubt to disapproval in a nanosecond. With a wave of her hand, the cloaked layer molded to Kushiel's form peeled back like a second skin, amorphous, tinged gray with streaks of black.

Seconds earlier the man sounded like everyone else in the room, but now, his voice held the same double-timbred tone and susurrated cadence as the first reaper I ever saw. The one who stood in the hospital doorway taunting me after George died.

"You knew the rules, Kushiel." Reggie shook her head. "We agreed all powers were to be muted before these proceedings commenced."

His response was a soft chittering sound at the back of his throat, and when he blinked, he flashed a horizontal nictitating membrane, same as the reaper from the hospital.

"You've left me no choice. You now have a strike against you for actions contrary to established dictates. Sanctions will be incurred and enforced after these proceedings are done."

Kushiel's fist struck the conference table. "And what about her?" He pointed at me.

"Me?" I replied, taken aback. "I'm neither an angel, nor a two legged reptile, unlike you. I have no powers to mute."

Reggie pulled out her chair with a loud scrape. The abrupt sound spoke volumes. Enough was enough. I agreed. I wanted this done and dusted as well, and the only way to do so was to make a start.

"Everyone sit," she instructed. "I hereby open these proceedings in my capacity as the Archangel of Judgment. Let the record reflect this is an informal preliminary inquest, and not a tribunal. Each party will speak during their allotted time, and *only* during that time unless a specific question is posed and requires rebuttal or response.

"This inquest will not devolve into commentator cacophony. There will be no talking over each other, *or* me. Failure to abide by the rules set in accordance with universal law will result in contempt of this inquiry, and possible dismissal." She eyed Kush particularly. "Is that understood?"

No one objected, so she nodded in response. "Good. I will begin with what we know to be true and undisputable. On the day in question, Louisa Jericho, and two others in the employ of Memento Mori, rescued Cade and Penny Praestes from where they were held against their will in physical form, separated from their respective souls. Is that correct?"

"Yes," I replied without hesitation.

One Scythe Fits All

"Objection." Kushiel tapped the end of his pencil on the table.

"To which part are you objecting?" The set of Reggie's brow would've made anyone think twice about interrupting. "These are the facts, Kush. Just because you don't like hearing them said aloud doesn't make them any less true. Cade is here now. Would you like him to verify for the record he was kidnapped by reapers and separated from his soul in the process?"

Kushiel made a face. "Withdrawn."

"The complaint against Louisa Jericho is that she employed reckless and unnecessary measures leading to lethal force in order to facilitate said rescue mission." Reggie looked at me again. "How do you plead?"

"Are you kidding me?" The tall, pixyish archangel was dead serious, and I must've sounded as stunned as I looked because she seemed taken aback by my reply.

"I'm very serious, Ms. Jericho. As should you be. The Angel of Death was already in transit with The Grim that morning. Morana had the power to banish her reapers or force them to stand down. You chose not to wait for them to arrive."

Kush made an ugly noise in his throat. "She's trigger happy. Who gifted her the ability to wield angel fire, anyway? Whoever they are, they are just as culpable and should be on trial as well."

"This is not a trial, Kush," Reggie reminded. "Stop summing up for the jury."

"Aren't you going to say anything?" I asked, holding Angelica's gaze with mine. "The adjudicator tagged you in this farce of an accusation. Surely you have something to say on the matter."

Reggie shook her head. "Unfortunately, Angelica cannot comment. The Angel of Death carries no weight in this inquest."

"That isn't fair. Was Angelica on her way? Where is the proof of that?" Cade chimed in, upset. "Louisa was the only one who cared enough to figure out where I was and who had my soul. If anyone is culpable, it's both sisters, for not paying enough attention to their own."

Angelica shot Cade a sharp look.

"Truth stings sometimes, Angie. You put too much on Louisa. You expected too much from her, too soon. As for Morana, we all know she ran her realm in absentia for eons, which is why she's in confinement cleaning up her mess."

I put my hand on his arm, stopping him from saying any more. "I know you're upset for me, but I did what I thought was right, based on the situation at hand. Not unlike identifying rogue reapers or handling unconventional spirit dives. You and Angie both know I listen to my gut. It hasn't failed me yet, even when I'm not the most—"

"Louisa!" Angelica's sharp tone ran at me like a knife, and I clamped my mouth shut. My mouth runneth over again, nearly handing the game to Kush by admitting I was a loose cannon who worked off script.

Reggie stifled a side smirk. "Angelica may have put too much on you as a fledgling Keeper, but it's clear she knew you had abilities as well as heart. As clear as it is that Cade can't be objective when it comes to you."

"I'm glad you all find this so amusing. Unfortunately, the facts remain as such," Kush interrupted. "Sixteen reapers were destroyed in seconds, not to mention the ones Ms. Jericho experimented on in the subway and other places before the morning in question. Her use of angel fire is an abomination. She is a human Keeper, and as such has no right to wield such power. It sets an unjust precedent and tips the balance of power too far to one side."

"I didn't ask for this so called gift," I shot back. "I don't even know how I developed the ability. It just…happened."

The words left my mouth resolute, but Kush made me question myself. Had I remembered it wrong? Was I reckless? Gripping Angelica's hand, I let the memory of that morning wash through me. Would she see what I saw? Did I really want her to if I was wrong?

One by one, reapers snaked from crevices in the rock face looking to surround us. They crept from the vines, their lizard-like eyes darting left and right.

Thea and Rose stayed behind me, each flanking my sides. Rose was right. There were sixteen in number.

We moved in a tight circle, the three of us keeping tabs on their advance. I fisted my pendant, feeling it gathering strength.

The sound of their claws scrabbling on the ground made my skin crawl as much as their stench, but I had to focus. One blink, one nose wrinkle, and it could be game over.

Their scales chittered like insects, in time with their jerky movements. One sprang to the trunk of the twisted tree, clinging to the bark. The others postured, their chittering fizz growing louder in the quiet.

"What are they waiting for?" Thea asked.

I shook my head. "I'm not sure. Maybe the one I fried in the subway warned them off and they're waiting for me to strike first."

White hot ice pressed at my chest, filling my core, and stilling my hot flashes. Every sinew blazed down to my Keeper's mark.

Rose screamed, and the sound jolted my focus. In that second a reaper sprang from its perch. It landed inches away, its foul breath in my face.

My mind blurred and instinct took over. Power coursed through my arms and down my legs, the same energy crackling through me as in the subway.

It consumed me, glowing like a nuclear core. I was ablaze. No conscious thought. No physical body. Just power.

The reaper screamed, its body incinerating with its proximity. I was the universe, and the universe was me. Infinite and resolute. I lifted my arms, circling Thea and Rose in the icy light.

The reapers screeched, scrabbling for the rockface, but it was too late. A ring of light blasted from me like a nuclear detonation, liquefying them where they stood...

"Louisa?" Reggie questioned.

One Scythe Fits All

"She's not even paying attention! You say it just happens," he restated dryly. "How convenient."

I swallowed hard. "Yes, it was damned convenient. Especially when my friends and I were outnumbered four to one by reapers. If memory serves, and mine serves me well, one of your reapers attacked first. One launched itself at me, landing inches from my face!"

"And what about the others?" His face wore a *gotcha* look. "They didn't attack, did they?"

Looking at this with an ice-cold eye, Kush's claims could be seen as valid. Were the other reapers in retreat, or were they regrouping for a more strategic attack to keep us away from the cave?

Either way, the angel fire had reached critical mass by then, and there was no stopping the fallout. Did that make me guilty? Should I have let that reaper punch a hole in my chest and yank out my soul? Should I have allowed its brethren to swarm Rose and Thea and do the same to them?

There was a military term for what happened. Collateral damage. Did it make me feel better knowing that? No. Was it preventable? That was the question.

Chapter Ten

"I WANT IT STATED FOR THE RECORD, Ms. Jericho has exhibited nothing less than a cavalier response to the death of so many of my brethren."

The Archangel of Judgment sighed. "For the last time, Kushiel. This is an inquiry, not a tribunal. Stop posturing. It serves no purpose here and it grates on my nerves. Quit it."

I had to stifle a smirk. "As I said, my actions were in self-defense. There is no way to view a reaper landing six inches from my face other than a material threat. As for the rest of your brethren, they circled in that same moment in attack position. What happened was a direct result of a hostile act on the part of the darkness. Reapers were guarding the cave where Cade's body and the object tethering his soul were concealed."

"And you expect this inquest to believe you just happened upon the ability to wield angel fire?" He raised both hands in a skeptical stance.

"Yes." I nodded emphatically. "I don't know where the ability came from or how it landed in my hands." I almost said literally, but then thought better of painting any more vivid a picture.

"Ms. Jericho," Reggie interrupted. "When did you first notice you had the ability to channel angel light?"

"When I witnessed a reaper attempting to snatch a soul from a living human. It was the subway incident Kushiel mentioned earlier, though he forgot that tidbit about his brethren when it came to souls still attached to living, breathing humans. The opposition claims my ability skews the balance of power between light and dark, yet their clawed fingers were snatching souls they had no right to. That is the very definition of skewing the balance of power."

"Where's the proof?" he shot back.

From the look on the pixie angel's face, even she knew that question was ridiculous. "Kush, it's well documented it took the Angel of Death and The Grim, working together, to restore souls snatched by your kind under the direction of Samyaza. Your argument holds no water. Move on."

"Thank you, Raguel." So far, the Archangel of Judgment seemed to be impartial. "It was *those* malicious acts, particularly the one I witnessed on the subway that triggered the angel fire. If reapers hadn't broken the compact between light and dark, none of this would have happened."

Kushiel fidgeted with his pencil. Had I stumped him? No. I made a valid argument, but his body language told me he weighed and discarded every possible turnabout to find a new tack.

"And what is the source of your newly acquired power?" he asked, with a new glint. "Explain to this inquiry how you wield your newly found power at will."

My forehead knotted until I had a unibrow. Hadn't he been paying attention? "I *don't* wield it at will. That's the whole point."

Reggie angled her head, her eyes probing. "Explain."

I lifted my hand, and Kush's dramatic gasp left everyone rolling their eyes. "I can't call the light to me, or activate it, or anything. It's not there, until it is. What I have noticed is there has to be a catalyst," I hesitated, not wanting to incriminate myself. "Something that triggers a need for it. I can only guess the angel fire is triggered by things that go against the balance." I shook my head. "I can't be any more specific, because I just don't know."

"And how do you sense that trigger?" Reggie queried further, and I swear Kush's nictitating eyes trailed to my chest.

I suspected they both knew the answer to that question, and the smug look on Kush's face told me he only needed my confirmation to move in for the kill.

One Scythe Fits All

This inquest had nothing to do with me wielding angel fire, nor did it have to do with sixteen dead reapers. This had everything to do with the secret weapon currently around my neck. The same secret weapon Yaz wanted and failed to obtain.

"I don't have an answer to that question," I replied with a shrug. "I don't sense triggers, nor do I seek them out. They just happen."

He sat up in his chair, clearly not expecting that for an answer. When in doubt dissemble, right?

"What about what happened on the day in question?" he sputtered. "You've already stated the trigger was the reaper who attacked you. A single reaper."

"That's just it." I didn't give him the chance to further his claim. "Your brethren were the trigger. What occurred that morning was a direct response to actions taken against me, Cade, Rose, and Penny. A karmic backlash."

I shrugged at his answering scoff. "You can sneer all you like. The fact remains I was simply a tool. A conduit used to reinstate the balance. I have no idea how it came to be. I don't control it, or command it. It just is. Much like the universe."

"So, you have delusions of grandeur now? Comparing yourself to the universe." He snorted.

I blinked at him and his sad attempt at gaslighting. "No. I am comparing angel fire to the universe. Not me."

"It doesn't matter." He tossed his pen to the table like dropping a mic. "You already incriminated yourself when you admitted to unorthodox means in conducting yourself as a Keeper."

Cade's hands hit the table. "That's a reach, and you know it."

Reggie banged her gavel, and Cade sat back in a huff. "Enoch, please strike that outburst from the record, and then read back Ms. Jericho's previous statement regarding use of unorthodox methods."

The scribe flipped pages until he paused to scroll one with his finger. "Ah, yes…here it is. *I know you're upset for me, but I did what I thought was right, based on the situation at hand. Not unlike identifying rogue reapers or handling unconventional spirit dives. You and Angie both know I listen to my gut. It hasn't failed me yet, even when I'm not the most…*" Enoch stopped with his finger still on the passage and looked up. "Shall I continue?"

"No. Thank you." Reggie waved him off. "Please continue with your recordkeeping."

The man flipped back to where he left off, and scribbled the last directive before nodding, his pencil at the ready.

"I stand by my claim," Kush summed up, clearly thinking he had made his case beyond a shadow of a doubt. "Louisa Jericho admitted to all and sundry her complete and utter disrespect for rules. She is a lone wolf. A reckless and mercenary creature given too much leash."

One Scythe Fits All

I wasn't someone's dog or any other pet, and didn't appreciate his analogy, but Reggie lifted her hand yet again. "In the read back, I heard one word. Unconventional. The same word could be used for you, Kushiel, arriving with your reaper side concealed, yet still in full force. The difference lies in the reasons one navigates within the unconventional.

"Ms. Jericho handles unconventional spirit dives in order to uncover the source tethering her charges to the earthly plane. Her goal is to free them to move on. YOU concealed and weaponized your nature in order to cause discomfort. The goal of which was to stack the odds in your favor. One reason, light. The other, dark. All I can say is at least you're consistent, Kush." She paused. "Your claim is, yet again, unfounded. Move on."

Kushiel jerked to his feet. "You know as well as I do, Raguel, the source of her abilities is that pendant!"

His hand shot up, pointing an accusing finger at my chest. "It's an illegitimate channel, and it needs to be destroyed. It already factors heavily in the death of sixteen reapers, and whether or not Ms. Jericho understood its power or not, its source or not, is not the issue at hand. Her own words incriminate her when she admits she is a conduit."

"That's ridiculous." Angelica broke her silence, shaking her head. "That pendant was a gift. I allow Louisa to wear it as a symbol of Keeper commitment and love. It's essence is light. Not power. Don't attach unfounded attributes to it, Kushiel. My brother unwisely tried that and is now walking the earthly plane fully human, with no recall as to his former self. Yaz was delusional, and neither I nor Morana know where that delusion stemmed from or who planted it. If anyone."

Reggie's eyes tracked to the spot where the pendant dangled hidden beneath my blouse. I knew she sensed it, same as Kush.

Having their eyes on my lady bits made me uncomfortable, even knowing it was the pendant's siren call that made them zero in on my covered cleavage.

I adjusted my suit jacket, trying for a redirect to move us past interest in the Keeper pendant. "I believe many concerns posed this afternoon could be clarified by the individual who called for this inquest. Don't you agree?"

Cade's eyes tracked both Reggie and Kush, and how neither seemed to hear me over the lure of the pendant. He smacked the flat of his hand on the conference room table, and the two actually jumped.

"The guilty party has to be Morana," his angry gaze clocked the adjudicator, managing the redirect I couldn't. "She's the most likely party. Her absenteeism and neglect cost her in more ways than one. Rogues with their own agendas. Reapers who went off script and broke the compact between light and dark. Who knows what else. It has to be The Grim."

Reggie's eyes dipped to the folder in front of her. It was open, but the documents faced the other way so I couldn't read what they said.

One Scythe Fits All

"Morana is under conservatorship." The adjudicator's statement was matter of fact. "There is no way she brought the charges."

She caught my eyes dipping to her notes and quickly closed the folder, which told me it wasn't Morana who called for this inquest. Whoever it was, Reggie wanted them under wraps.

"The Grim may be under conservatorship, but that means nothing, really," I began again, taking a different tack. "Like any crime boss, it's not unfathomable to run a syndicate from behind bars. John Gotti did so before his death. Warren Jeffs still does, although his isn't as much crime syndicate as it is cult, but that's six of one, half dozen of another.

"Both men are examples of criminals running things from jail. The Grim is savvy. No one can deny that about Morana. She could easily manipulate the balance of light and dark under her conservator's nose."

Angelica reached to slide the file closer, but the adjudicator was quick to snatch it back.

"Why are you protecting the accuser's identity? They filed charges against one of *my* Keepers." Angelica was pulling rank. Or she was about to.

"I'm not." Reggie ran a hand through her pixie cut, and the move disclosed her incandescence. I guess angels *could* cloak their glow.

"Raguel, c'mon." Angie wasn't having it.

The adjudicator fidgeted with the edge of the folder. Was she torn about not showing it to Angelica? She was leading this inquiry, so her hands were tied.

Especially with Kush eyeballing her now. If Reggie showed even a hint of preference, it would taint the proceedings, and not in my favor.

"Morana isn't a crime boss, nor is she in jail," Reggie replied finally. "She was not the one who raised the questions and called for a preliminary inquest."

I understood Reggie's predicament, but I still had a right to know my accuser. "In the human realm, the accused has rights. I can't imagine it would be different here."

Angelica's eyes took on a silver sheen, and that gleam told me I had hit on something. "Louisa is correct, Reggie. It's universal law. The accused has the right to know their accuser." She held out her hand for the file, and Reggie spared a glance for Enoch, still hesitating.

"I'm serious, Raguel." Angie wasn't playing with the Archangel of Judgment. "Don't make me summon Michael."

The adjudicator pressed her lips together, exhaling through her nose, and Kush sat back in his chair with a chuckle.

"Care to let the rest of us in on the joke, pencil neck?" My insult was ill-timed, especially when Angelica stood from her chair, knocked for six.

"I don't believe it." The note of shock in the Angel of Death's voice stretched the knots in my stomach to near strangulation.

The adjudicator held out the file, and Kush grinned, chewing on the end of his pencil. "Read it and weep."

One Scythe Fits All

Angie opened the file, scanning the documents and the adjudicator's notes. When she looked up, her expression said it all. I was screwed.

"For crap's sake! What does it say?" My blurt prompted Angie to read the pertinent part aloud.

"A preemptive recommendation was drafted ahead of these proceedings. The recommendation is for Louisa Jericho to be temporarily grounded while inquest findings are deliberated. For a probationary status to be in effect until all inquiries are complete, and a decision is rendered as to the need for a formal tribunal. This temporary grounding will be effective immediately after the preliminary inquiry is closed."

Aghast, I blinked, unable to speak.

"A tribunal," Cade repeated warily. "What does that mean for us going forward?"

Angelica closed the file. Her mouth was more of a slash than ever. "If a tribunal is deemed necessary, it will decide Louisa's fate."

"My fate?" I croaked half in disbelief, half in growing anger.

She nodded. "If a tribunal is called, they will hear the facts of the case and determine whether or not you remain a Keeper. If they decide on you being sent down, from there they decide whether or not you return to your human state or move on."

I stared at them unblinking at this point. I had been thrown into being a Keeper with no warning and no real training. I had no frame of reference for anything, only a baptism by fire and my own gut. If mistakes were made, they were due to extenuating circumstances.

What would my life look like if I was no longer a Keeper? It wasn't that long ago I had no idea about Keepers and reapers, or that they were real and ever present. So why was it so hard to imagine going back to that ignorant bliss?

No more hot flashes. No ghosts wandering my yard or my roof. No icy hot infernos blasting through my body. No chittering reapers. No witnessing a person's last moments. No heartbreaks. Maybe being sent down wasn't such a bad thing after all.

I went to open my mouth, but Angelica yanked me by the arm. "This entire situation is as unacceptable as it is unfair, and I will make my displeasure known. As far as that written recommendation, I will take it under advisement, and if he shows himself anytime soon, I'll yank that sword from his hand and use it to shish kabab his balls! You can tell him that's a promise from ME!"

My jaw hit the table. I hadn't put two and two together. "It was Michael who brought charges against me?" I looked first to Reggie, and then Angelica. "Michael. As in Archangel, a.k.a. Sword of God."

Reggie slid the case file back before tucking it into her briefcase. Her expression was as resolute as when we first entered the room. "I think some clarity needs to be interjected before we jump to conclusions. Michael did NOT bring charges against you, Ms. Jericho. He suggested this inquiry to determine the scope of your abilities, and how to move forward from there. Whether you believe so or not, that recommendation was written to protect you.

"He doesn't believe you should have the ability to wield his light. The flaming sword is his domain. He's the one who determines where it strikes and when. Your ability to tap into his light stash is not only unusual, it could be undermining. You're not an angel, Ms. Jericho. Wielding angelic light was not meant for humankind. It has the power to consume, to corrupt both in body and mind."

Reggie's words hit like a ton of bricks. Maybe Michael was concerned for my safety, or maybe he never learned to share, but one thing was crystal clear—someone else piggybacked his inquiry for ulterior motives. The question was who and why.

"If Michael didn't bring charges, and his only reason for this inquiry was to question and counsel my abilities and my welfare, then what is pencil neck doing here?" I jerked my thumb toward Kush. "How did the darkness get involved?"

Reggie slid her eyes to Kush, and her face looked like she sucked on a lemon. "The other side got wind there was to be an inquiry and is making the most of it."

That was all I needed to hear. I refused to be a human ping pong ball, batted back and forth in a game between light and dark.

"You know what?" I got to my feet, nearly knocking my chair over. "Ground me. I'll consider it a vacation, and if it's decided I can't be a Keeper anymore, then so be it. I'll live my life with Cade and never give this crazy train a second thought."

"Louisa."

Angelica's tone was a warning, but Reggie lifted a hand to interrupt. "Ms. Jericho, you have every right to be upset, but you're missing the point. If this goes south, you won't be able to give this crazy train a second thought because you won't remember any of this or your time as a Keeper, and that includes Cade."

Her words stopped my rant cold, and I looked at Cade. He sat so quietly in his chair, but his face told me he understood the implications the moment Angelica read the recommendation. If this inquest led to a tribunal, it was a lose-lose scenario. For me. For him. For us.

I shook my head as if clearing a bad dream. The prospect of losing the love of my life was unthinkable.

"Surely the universe wouldn't separate soulmates over something like this." My eyes searched Reggie's face, and then Angelica's, completely ignoring Kush.

"Let's hope it doesn't get to that point," the Archangel of Judgment replied, and I swallowed hard, realizing that was the best she could offer.

"*Uhm*," Kush interrupted. "About that pendant—"

I shot him a death look shutting him up, but Reggie took the dismissal even further. "As per usual, Kushiel, your capacity for churlishness knows no bounds. That will be in my report along with sanctions for your earlier disregard."

"With the Archangel of Judgment's permission, I'd like to make a statement as well." I waited a moment for any objections. "If the Angel of Death deems it necessary, I will give the pendant to her, and ONLY her. From there, she may do with it as she pleases."

I shouldn't have had to make a statement at all, but I wanted one on the record so there was no question later.

My brain was on overload at this point, so I pushed my chair back from the table, but not before nailing Kush's smug face with a final glare…for now.

Chapter Eleven

RAGUEL'S GAVEL BANGED, ending the preliminary inquest. My knees went soft at the sound, and Cade's steadying hand found my elbow.

"Easy there, killer." He stood from his chair, slipping his arm firmly around my waist. "I think it's safe to say round one belongs to us."

"Maybe you shouldn't call me killer. I know it's an endearment, but the other side might get ideas." My eyes found his, and it was all I could do not to burst into frustrated tears.

Cade cupped my cheek, wiping escaped wetness away with his thumb. "I think Kushiel has other things to worry about right now." He cocked his head toward Angelica. "It looks like Big Ange is locked and loaded, and Kush is feeling the burn from across the room."

One Scythe Fits All

The Angel of Death unleashed an unblinking glare on Kushiel, and the man suddenly looked like he needed a bathroom asap.

I couldn't help the cold satisfaction at seeing the smarmy reptile squirm under the intensity of her stare. It was just what I needed.

Angie broke contact with the reaper, and Kushiel slumped into his chair, wiping his face with a handkerchief. She held the squeeze just long enough for the cockroach to feel the heat for days.

"Huh." Angelica sniffed her approval. "Who knew turning the tables was such fun. Now one reaper knows what it's like to sweat in *your* presence."

"Poetic justice, Ange." Cade gave Kush a mock salute. "Well done."

I blinked the last of my stress tears away. "Poetic or not, at this point I'll take any kind of justice."

"Listen to me, Louisa." Angelica took my hand, her grip tight. "Probation or not, we take today as a win. Next step, we find a top dominion defender. Just in case."

"Dominion?" I asked.

"It's an abbreviation for a certain celestial tribunal. The formal title is the Court of Powers and Dominion. Hence a dominion defender."

I slipped my hand from hers, hoping I didn't offend. "I'm confused. I thought Raguel said she'd take the case."

Angelica spared a glance for the adjudicator as she stood with Enoch over his transcripts. "Reggie is good, but I saw her eyes when she tracked your pendant, and that alone gives me pause. We'll discuss this further, but not here. Clarence has probably paced a rut in the grass by now. It's time to go home."

The jolt of satisfaction at seeing Kushiel squirm was fleeting, especially after walking through that unending waiting room and its vast empty feeling on our way to the revolving doors.

I knew the administrative purpose of this building, and that processing the dead in limbo was an atlas-sized feat, but the weight of that desolation only compounded the events of the day.

I couldn't breathe. We were barely through the front courtyard when I ripped my jacket from my shoulders. Buttons from my blouse flew in every direction, leaving me in just my camisole.

"Lou?" Cade stopped me before we hit the grass, his stance like he confronted a feral animal.

"I'm fine, Cade."

"Really? You're standing in a torn blouse, looking like you're about to hyperventilate. That doesn't sound fine."

"I'm frustrated and I'm scared, but promise, I'm fine. I just needed to feel like me, and that's not a business suit. Stop looking at me like I'm ready to jump."

"I think that's part of the plan." Angelica gestured to Clarence waiting on the slope for us. "Unless you want to stick around limbo a little longer."

One Scythe Fits All

Her joke wasn't lost on me, and I smirked. "I think my snarky side is rubbing off on you."

"Lou, are you sure you're okay?" Cade was like a dog with a bone. "I know what you're like when you feel cornered, and this is the mutha of all corners."

"Mutha?" I laughed at his attempt at slang. "Guess I'm negatively influencing you, too."

"Leave her alone, Cade. Louisa needs time to process. She's fine."

Angelica said I was fine, but I knew she saw through my cover. Anxiety-laced adrenaline fueled a need to run and not stop until I collapsed.

I wanted familiar noise. Car horns in traffic and the rumble and squeal of the subway. At the same time, I wanted peace. My mind churned, reiterating everything said today.

Without warning, I did an about face and rushed down the slope past Clarence toward the water's edge. Cade didn't follow, and I was sure it had more to do with a certain angel's Vulcan death grip than Cade's willingness to give me space.

Standing on the pitched grass, I watched the sunset over the waves. The whitecaps out in deeper water paled to soft, lapping strokes on the loamy shore below. I sat in the warm grass with my arms locked around my knees.

If things went south, would my soul remember Cade somewhere deep inside? Or would this cause a soul scar so intense I'd carry it into the afterlife?

"Honey, you've got the same expression on your face you had whenever I said I didn't want to move in with you."

My head jerked around so quickly I nearly ruptured a vertebrae. "Emmie?" I blinked, not trusting my senses.

"In the flesh. Or a facsimile thereof close enough to hug." She smiled, and her face crinkled in a familiar cross between Mrs. Claus and Yoda.

She held her arms out to me, and I scrambled to my feet, slipping on the grass. "Even in limbo, you're still my clumsy girl."

I bundled into her arms, breathing in the familiar mix of cherry blossoms and chocolate. Cherry blossoms from her favorite scent, and chocolate from, well…chocolate. A vice we both shared. Chocolate was life, and for me, chocolate croissants were bliss.

Hugging her hard, I squeezed back tears. If this was some sort of celestial memory projection, it was a damn good one.

"Good God, Louie Belle. Be careful or you'll crush the old girl's bones."

I opened my eyes. "George?" My knees gave out. Hanging onto Emmie, I slid to the grass again.

"Who'd you expect? Clark Gable?" He laughed and his familiar wheezy chuckle hurt my heart.

I blinked again, watching him slip an arm around Em's shoulders. "Did you didn't think I'd let anyone keep me away from my girl? I made it very clear when I marched up to that inert window up yonder."

One Scythe Fits All

He yanked a thumb toward the administrative building at the top of the slope. "Emmie was a damn good Keeper, and she kept Memento Mori's secret centuries. I told them the old girl deserved compensation, and that didn't include waiting in endless lines."

"Obviously, they listened to you," I said, shocked, but Em shook her head.

"Not a chance, honey, but it was fun to watch Georgie tilt at celestial windmills."

"Fun?" When he flashed his block-toothed, Cheshire cat grin that reminded me of Ernest Borgnine, I wasn't sure I could bear it.

"But you're together, right? And you're not stuck waiting forever in that building." I paused. Or were they? Maybe this was some sort of reprieve because I had been called to limbo and was having a rough time.

Guilt bit at my gut.

"I know that look, too." Em held her hand out to help me up, but I shook my head. I could get to my feet on my own. "You have nothing to feel guilty about, honey."

"Am I the reason you two are still stuck in limbo?"

Emmie laughed at that, and the sound both warmed and scolded. "You spend too much time worrying about everyone else. It's time to be a little selfish. George and I are together, and no, we're not stuck in any mindless queue. In fact, we have a little house on the other side of the bridge."

I followed her line of sight, catching a wink of pretty cottages nestled into a ridge on the far shore.

"It's small, but very cozy for just us two. We even have a garden and a gorgeous view of the water."

Georgie nodded. "Angelica came through for Emmie, even though she was upset the old girl never got around to telling you about Memento Mori."

Angie really was an angel, in all senses of the word. Cade told me not to worry after George died. He said Angelica would take care of him as a favor to Emmie, and she was good to her word. They weren't in paradise, but they were together, and they seemed happy.

"I'm glad she took care of you. Lord knows I've been going by the seat of my pants since Em..." I let my words trail, and both Emmie and George laughed.

"You don't have to pussy foot around us, Lou. We know we bought the farm. That was our mortal life, but there's a reason the afterlife is called the *afterlife*." He smiled again. "It's still life. Just in a different form."

In a flash they both looked my age, and seconds later, the two were little kids together, chuckling at the stunned look I must've had on my face.

"We're happy, Louisa, and we want you to be, too," Emily said, flashing back to her present age, complete with long silver braids.

George nodded. "You're stronger than you know, Lou. Why else do you think I called you my Louie Belle Slugger?"

"We're always with you, honey. Even if you can't feel us anymore." Her eyes moved to the pendant hanging in the open above my camisole. "Don't forget, you've got a piece of me very close to your heart. It's where you need to look to help fix what's happening."

"You know about my inquest?" I couldn't have been more stunned.

George nodded. "We know, and it's a travesty. There's more at play here than meets the eye, Lou. You need to think outside the box to find the answer on this one. Don't fall for Occam's Razor."

My forehead crinkled. "Did anyone send you to tell me that?"

Em and George shared a look. "We're not supposed to be here, but your hurt and frustration was too hard to ignore. You need help, and knowing what we know, you're not going to get it from celestial channels. You think humans have a monopoly on bureaucracy? You should see it up close and personal from our vantage point."

"I'm confused. Angelica came through for you, and she's been there for me plenty since I took over as Keeper. She's on my side. As is Cade." If Emmie and George were stuck in limbo, was it like the movie *Groundhog Day* where they lived the same thing over and over again?

Mentioning Cade brought a crinkly smile to both their faces, and George pulled Em closer into a side hug. "Now that one's a keeper." Emmie nodded. "In every sense of the word. Don't let go of him, Lou. He's your forever."

I couldn't wait to tell him what Em said, but at the same time I couldn't wrap my mind around the rest.

"I have to ask in blunt terms. Are you two telling me Angie is not my ally?"

They shared a look again, and my stomach knotted. "She's your ally, Lou," Georgie replied, "but she's also an angel. A high level celestial. She may be forced to choose, and we're not sure if that choice will be you."

"George is right." Em's face looked pained, but she nodded anyway. "That's why we're breaking the rules in telling you to look beyond the obvious. To think with your head and your heart and to follow your gut. That little piece of me is a clue, as are the others."

Em eyeballed the pendant again, and this time I got the feeling she hadn't overtly pointed to it for a reason. Was she afraid someone was watching?

"I miss you both so much, I wish I could conjure you from time to time. Just to talk. To hang out. To attend my wedding." My teasing grin ebbed. If things went south there wouldn't be a wedding.

"No!" Emmie shook her head hard enough her braids wobbled. "I won't let you do that to yourself. I told you. That man is your forever. In this life, and all the afterlives to come. YOU have to see that through with him."

The air changed around us. It shimmered, growing slightly colder and I knew my time with them had come to an end.

"I love you both so very much." I didn't waste a second on the how or why of them being in limbo when

One Scythe Fits All

I had thought they moved on. I simply gathered them to me for a last hug.

"We love you, too, Louie Belle." George squeezed me back, and the two of us nearly crushed Em between us. "Just heed what the old girl said, okay?"

I nodded. "I will."

"Honey, that little piece of me is the reason Georgie and I are here. Angelica made it happen for him, but I'm here because of a certain choice I made." She shrugged, not elaborating on her thought.

I didn't need her to. She was stuck in limbo because a piece of her soul was part and parcel of the pendant mosaic around my neck. She, along with other Keepers.

George and Emmie stepped back from me, and the wind picked up. It blew so wildly, I had to shield my eyes. When it finally died down, I lowered my arm only to find me sitting on the grass in the same spot I had been earlier. Had I imagined their whole visit?

A gentle breeze tickled my hair, and I caught the scent of cherry blossoms and chocolate, and I smiled. Their visit was real.

"Lou?" Cade's voice called me from behind, and I turned.

"C'mon," I said, patting the grass beside me. "Sit. The view is amazing." I would tell him about Emmie and George and everything they said, but not now, and definitely not here.

"We need to go, Lou. Clarence is getting antsy, and I really want to get you home." He held his hand out to help me up, pulling me into a hug. "Are you sure you're okay?" he asked, sniffing my hair. "Why do you smell like cherry and chocolate?"

Chapter Twelve

CADE AND I SAT AT MY kitchen counter, both ravenous. Angie said we might be after the jump back to the earthly plane, and she wasn't kidding. We ordered enough food to feed a small army, and the two of us alone made a dent that could choke a horse.

It was late. Time and space did not hold up well when reentering our dimension. As far as the day went, we spent the afternoon in limbo, but when we got back it wasn't just nightfall. It was nightfall three days hence.

Thea had left at least thirty text messages and voicemails on my cell phone. When I called her to let her know Cade and I were back, I thought she'd hex our private parts for making her worry.

Still, I finally got her to understand we had no idea, and that Angie would probably give her hazard pay for holding down the brownstone and its ghostly squatters while we were gone. Of course, I had to promise she could come over in the morning. Until she saw for herself that Cade and I were in one piece both mentally and physically, we'd have no peace.

"I saw Emmie and George when we were in limbo. They look great, by the way."

Cade nearly choked on his mouthful of sesame chicken. I dropped my fork, reaching to hand him a wad of paper napkins. "Are you okay?"

He nodded, coughing, and then reached for his beer, but I shot up from the counter to get him some water.

Handing him the glass, I took the beer bottle from his other hand. "I'm not explaining to city EMTs why you smell like brewery while choking."

He took a large gulp of water and then exhaled, sputtering a little more. "You sound like my mother."

"From the 1880s?" I laughed, putting his beer next to his plate. "I don't think so. Maybe if I took a switch to your backside after taking the beer from your hand, that would be more likely."

He chuckled, wiping his mouth. "Mama was definitely a hard nut to crack, but she would've liked you. She appreciated women with spirit."

"And I've got spirit to spare. Just look out the backdoor window."

That earned me a wry smirk and a wink. "Not what I meant, but true enough."

"In all the time we've spent together and the obstacles we've faced, you never really talk about your life before you became a Keeper."

A small frown furrowed the line above his eyes. "I told you about my family."

"You told me you come from a family of Keepers, and that you knew from a young age you'd follow your great granny into the family business," I paused, "but you haven't said a word about anyone else. I'm going to make a leap of faith and assume you had a full human life before you became a Keeper."

He put his water glass down and picked up his bottle of beer again. Looking at me over the long neck's rim, he pursed his lips as though weighing what to say. "Are you asking me about the women in my past?"

Heat bloomed in my face. He wasn't wrong. I had hinted as much, so why was I suddenly embarrassed? Cade and I had been through so much in such a short time, I didn't think the thought of him with anyone else would bother me.

"From the tinge of color staining your cheeks, I'm guessing I guessed correctly. You want to know if I was ever intimately involved. The answer is yes. As you delicately put it, I led a full human life. I had a wife, and three children before I became a Keeper. The story isn't a happy one, and I have no descendants to watch over from a distance. The Spanish Flu took care of that for me."

Floored by the raw honesty of his answer, I didn't know what to say. I was a mouth almighty idiot. Especially since he explained the lot of a Keeper's life.

Keepers usually lead a lonely life. Everyone we love ages and eventually dies, but we stay.

Those were Cade's words when he babysat me during the two weeks Angelica gave me to make up my mind. If I had taken five seconds to think before I opened my mouth…heat still burned in my cheeks, but now it was from shame instead of nosy curiosity.

"I'm so sorry, Cade. I shouldn't have asked." I swallowed the lump of regret in my throat.

He reached across the table for my hand. "It's okay, love. Questions are part of the package in any intimate relationship, even more so when the man you love has lived multiple lifetimes. Our situation isn't exactly typical." He kissed my fingertips. "You get a pass. This time. Next time you want to know something, just ask. It doesn't pay for us to pussyfoot around each other."

I didn't know what to say. I didn't see regret in his face. Nostalgia, yes. A tinge of sadness, perhaps, but no pain. Time really did heal all wounds, or maybe it just dimmed sad memories and with them our hurt.

The city echoed outside while I waited for our awkward silence to pass. The rest of that original conversation ran through my head. Ironic, really. When Emmie died, I was caught in a triangle. Not something juicy like a threesome. No. A metaphysical triangle. Life as I knew it against the life of a Keeper against

Emmie's afterlife. The question begged then, where did I belong?

This new deck of cards had dealt up another triangle of sorts. The life I knew as a Keeper against the verdict of a possible tribunal against a life with or without Cade.

If this wasn't so serious, I'd laugh at the irony. The universe didn't play when it handed out hard choices. Four months ago, I had Emmie's fate in my hands. At least that was something I could control. I was used to taking on responsibility for others. But this? I had no control whatsoever, and that set my teeth and my every last nerve on edge.

Was I a control freak? A bit. A lot. Okay, fine. My name is Louisa, and I am a complete control freak. Cade gave me a pass for beating around the bush, but I think I get a pass for this new triangle conundrum. I think I'd rather have to choose between two guys, than two existences. One, because neither is a fair choice, and two, this forces Cade to have to choose as well. In this instance, the universe and all its celestial hierarchies sucked the big one.

"I can't believe you saw Emmie and George." Cade dove into his sesame chicken again. "Of all the things you could've blurted, that was the very last thing I expected."

"We were in limbo, so I guess anything is possible when you're across the veil."

He chewed, considering. "True, but why were they in limbo? Angelica promised she'd take care of George for Emmie's sake, so I suppose I assumed that meant them moving on together. Not stuck in the in between, waiting in a queue together."

"They aren't in a queue. They live in limbo. Apparently, Angelica gave them a cottage overlooking the bay." I chewed quietly, watching him process. "They weren't supposed to interact with me. There's some rule or something, but neither Emily nor George were much for following rules. They had a lot to say about me, about the situation I'm in now…" I waited a breath. "About you."

"Me?" He stopped with a forkful halfway to his mouth.

I told him what they said. About him being my forever. That we had a fight on our hands in order to claim that forever. About Angie stuck between her own rock and a hard place, and us having to think outside the box to find resolutions to all of the above.

He put his fork down and sat back in his chair. It was a lot to digest, and I had to give him the chance to absorb it before continuing.

"They said we have to fight to be together?" He angled his head, regarding me. "Sounds rather retrospective considering what we've already battled."

"Why do you sound so surprised to hear we're soulmates? Residing in limbo, George and Emmie happen to be in the know." I reached for the carton of fried rice.

"I'm not surprised at that at all."

"Then what made me almost have to do the Heimlich maneuver on you?"

One Scythe Fits All

He chewed another forkful.

"It's their doubts about Angelica, isn't it? You didn't seem too concerned about her feelings when you threw her under the bus at the start of the inquest."

"That was different."

"Why? Because it was about me?"

"Exactly."

"But this is still about me. About us. I'm still in the hot seat until they decide if there's enough probable cause to merit a tribunal."

Cade put his fork down and then wiped his mouth, the whole while watching me. "What if we both cashed in our chips? What if we went to Angelica and asked to move on, but the stipulation would be we moved on together. She already set the precedent with Emmie and George, so it's not that far of a stretch."

"She'd never agree to it, Cade." I spooned more food onto my plate. "First off, you're well over a century older than me. Secondly, you're one of only a handful of level five Keepers, and before you say I am as well, you know damn well that was payback."

"That was a well-earned reward, Lou. Not compensation."

"You're her most trusted asset. Besides, I don't want to move on. I want to live our lives the way we planned, together."

I toyed with twirling lo mein noodles around my dish. "I think we need to do what Emily said and think outside the box. There's something we're missing, and I think it's because we're too close to the problem."

He sat back in his chair, taking a sip from his bottle of beer. "What do you suggest then? Distance?"

"Not distance. Perspective. We need to take a step back. Work together but give the little grey cells a chance to percolate."

"Like another vacation?"

I shook my head. "You're still thinking distance. Emmie kept eyeing my pendant when she said think outside the box. We know Kushiel framed his entire argument to get me to say the pendant was the source of my abilities."

"True. But what does that have to do with Emmie?"

I lifted a hand, nonplussed. "That's just it. I'm not sure. I'm pretty sure Emily is still in limbo because her soul isn't intact. Angelica basically said as much. Not about Emmie in particular, but she said limbo was for souls in wait in, and that sometimes there were questions, or extenuating circumstances that needed further investigation before they could move on."

"I'm not trying to be thick, but what does Emmie's soul situation have to do with charges leveled against you by the darkness?" Cade asked, getting back to the point.

I gestured with my fork. "I don't know that it has anything to with the charges. Right now, they seem to be two separate things, but we also thought Penny's soul in a spirit box had nothing to do with rogue reapers, and we were wrong. After today, I believe even more this inquest was a smoke screen to get to something bigger. Something juicier."

One Scythe Fits All

"By juicier you mean your pendant."

"Perhaps." I paused. "Think about it, Cade. Reggie admitted Michael's aim wasn't a tribunal. He wanted an investigation into the source of my newfound power. He had various reasons, one of which was the nature of angel fire itself. Its all-consuming nature."

"I'm listening."

"Reggie said angel fire could affect the mind. Now that I've had a chance to process, I think I know what she meant."

"What?"

"Angel fire took control of me that morning in the botanical gardens, and I lost myself to it. It's poetic to say I was one with the universe and the universe one with me, but..." I scratched my head, trying to remember. "It's a blur now, and perhaps that's by design. Still, I remember someone…maybe Thea…reaching out to grab me, and someone else yanking her back, saying not to touch me. That it was me, but not."

Cade sat forward in his chair. Concern and fascination warred on his face. "Why didn't you ever say?"

"Like I said, it's all a blur. Maybe it's trauma, or maybe I'm only recalling it now because Reggie reignited the memory."

"Is Kushiel correct? Could your pendant be the source?"

I shrugged. "I don't know, but I don't think so. I'm a conduit. Of that I'm sure. Whether or not the pendant reacts to me or me to it is the million-dollar question."

His gaze dropped to the teardrop shaped mosaic at my chest. "How can one piece of jewelry carry that much sway?"

"Who knows? Even Reggie had a reaction enough to make Angelica think twice about her taking our side in a tribunal."

He nodded, frowning. "I saw. It was as if she was in thrall."

"Holy crow, Cade." I chuckled, shaking my head. "I'm Gollum."

"Who?"

"Gollum," I repeated, as if he should know. "From the *Lord of the Rings* trilogy? My precious?" I laughed again. *"We wants it, we needs it... They stole it from us. Sneaky hobbitses. Wicked. Tricksy..."*

"Should I be worried you do that creepy voice so well?"

I waved him off. "Forget that. The point is the characters chased the ring of power, but only those who possessed it risked it changing them forever. Changing them for the worse. It consumed them. It messed with their minds."

Cade leaned back in his chair again. "I know we're talking hypothetical correlations, but the ring of power was created to oppress. Your pendant was created for the greater good. You use it for good."

"Then maybe I'm not Gollum. Maybe I'm Frodo. His character resisted the ring of power until it could be destroyed to save Middle Earth."

"I think you're getting a little carried away, Lou. Your geeky side is really showing. The earthly plane is not in danger of being destroyed."

He missed what I meant by a mile. The earthly plane was not in jeopardy, but the balance between light and dark might be.

"Cade, what if this has nothing to do with me per say, and everything to do with owning something that can be weaponized."

"You're talking angel fire."

I nodded. "Kushiel presented himself as this powerful prosecutor, but what if he's just the fall guy for the darkness? His job was to get me to admit the pendant was my channel into Michael's light. That admission would condemn me and put the pendant at risk. Risk to be destroyed, or more likely, risk to be stolen.

"You were still entombed inside the cave when Yaz tried for a power grab before Michael took him down. He tried to take the pendant from me, and the more I think about it, the more I believe Yaz was a patsy. Even Morana was affected by the pendant. She tried to snatch it as well, but Angelica smacked her back."

"Jesus."

"Maybe…just maybe, the darkness truly believes this pendant is something they can manipulate and use."

Cade knew what I meant without me having to spell it out. The world wasn't at risk for destruction, but there was a powerplay between light and dark with the balance at stake.

He got up from the counter to pace in front of the back door. The roman shade was down, and I was glad the ghosts were respecting our interior boundaries. Either that, or Thea reinforced the wards while we were gone.

"Lou…" Cade stopped pacing, and his face was adamant. "You have to give the pendant to Angelica. We need to tell her what we think is happening."

"No, Cade. I made it very clear I would willingly give Angie the pendant, but only if she deems it necessary."

"She will deem it necessary once we tell her what we just discussed."

I shook my head. "She's going to want proof, Cade. Not speculation. No matter how feasible and informed.

"Fine. Then we'll give her the pendant for safekeeping. If someone tries to pull shenanigans, better it happen on Angie's watch than ours."

He was in protective mode again, and I loved him for it, but my gut told me now was not the time to give Angie or anyone else the pendant. I hadn't connected the dots yet, but I knew there was a parallel to the charges laid at my feet.

"We can give the pendant to Angelica once we figure out why the darkness wants to control angel fire."

One Scythe Fits All

"I think that's pretty obvious, don't you? They want mutually assured destruction. A celestial cold war standoff. Thankfully you didn't mention your banded connection to the universal divine or we'd have reapers crawling all over this house trying to get to you."

Cade's words struck a chord. Not the part about the darkness wanting a celestial cold war. There was something about crawling reapers that pinged my mind.

"I think we need to backtrack a bit," I suggested, thinking aloud. "We need better perspective. Thea is coming in the morning. We can head to Memento Mori together, and then hit the archives. With the three of us putting our heads together, something's gotta give. I'll have the pendant with me, and if Angie wants it, I'll give it to her then. If not, what safer place to be for a reaperific secret weapon than Death Central?"

Chapter Thirteen

THE SUBWAY JOLTED ITS WAY UPTOWN toward the 59th Street station. The lights flickered in and out, and I watched Cade's protective vibe shift into overdrive with every squeal and rattle.

He wasn't happy about the three of us risking public transportation, but I assured him reapers would rather eat their young than risk running into me.

"Were you really grounded?" Thea asked, watching Cade watch everyone else in the subway car. "It's like he's anticipating a Crocodile Dundee, 'That's not a knife…THIS is a knife!' scenario."

"He's gone into caveman Keeper mode ever since Raguel clipped my wings." I snorted a chuckle. "Can you imagine? The celestial set would lose their minds if they thought I was a covert angel."

One Scythe Fits All

She tightened her strap-hanger grip as the car bumped around a curve. "Louisa Jericho. Librarian by day, celestial spy by night."

I shushed her. "Don't even joke."

"I could do an obscure scry if you want. With so many layers to everything at Memento Mori, I've been practicing with arcane methods. I would need a drop of your blood to do so, but I bet I could find the source of why you suddenly found yourself a conduit for Michael's you know what."

"You make it sound almost dirty."

She laughed. "You've seen that boy. Archangel or not, it's not hard to imagine his you know what. He's packing."

"Ugh. Now I can't unsee it."

"Imagine what we could see with a drop of HIS blood. You've got Cade, and the two of you were built for speed, but my curves were built for bouncing."

Thea never dealt in blood magic, so my raised eyebrow was not unexpected.

"Quit looking at me like I've broken some cosmic cardinal rule. Morally gray sometimes requires morally gray. When it comes to blood, a little drop goes a long way."

The subway squealed, telling us our stop was ahead. We'd get off on Lexington Avenue and then walk to Madison and Death Central.

"Is Angelica expecting us?" Thea asked, moving to stand by the subway car doors.

"No, but I don't think she'll have a problem with us spending time in the archive." I moved to stand with her, motioning for Cade to do so as well.

Thea shrugged. "I suppose it's no big deal. An archive is tantamount to a dusty library, and who gets in trouble in the library?"

"Are you forgetting the outbreak of STDs at the local senior center from hookups in the stacks at *our* library? Don't you remember Alistair's red face when the Jefferson was dubbed a place for books and hooks?

She giggle-snorted a laugh at that.

"Do I want to know?" Cade asked.

"Not unless you want a crash course on senior citizens doing the nasty against a shelf of dusty leather bounds."

He made a face. "I'm going to assume you mean books when you say leather bounds."

"Do I, though?" Thea winked.

I never saw Cade so relieved as when the intercom announced our stop and the doors slid open.

We stepped out onto the platform and then up to street level. Memento Mori was four short blocks away. One over and three up, so we walked in relative quiet, enjoying the crisp October air.

"Cade…" Thea broke the quiet.

"Nope." He shook his head. "I have my own brand of kink. I don't need to hear about your leather bounds."

I choked on a sip from my travel cup. "You two are killing me."

"I knew it!" Thea clicked the inside of her cheek. "Girl, I hope you know how lucky you are."

"I do," I replied, slipping my arm through Cade's elbow.

"I do have a question, though, and it's not about Keeper kink. From listening to you guys talk, I know Keepers are all human with special perks."

"And?"

She looked across at me as we walked. "What about reapers? Are they created, or are they born? Or were they once human, as well?"

I could've answered her question, but I decided to let Cade do it. "It's not really complicated, Thea. First off, despite our perks, Keepers are *still* human, even if our mortality has been suspended. So, that's a misconception there. Reapers are mostly entities created by Abaddon, a.k.a. the Angel of the Abyss. He's the beast who resides in the lowest pit of Hell.

"Millenia ago, there was debate as to whether or not Abaddon ruled the darkness, but that was set straight. The ruler of Hell is Samael. He's the one who lords over Lucifer, and Satanael, a.k.a. Satan, as well as the other princes of Hell. Reapers are service demons, and Morana is their boss, but she answers to the big bad and his hierarchy of fallen angels.

"Reapers aren't exclusively entities, though. Some humans make the choice to become reapers. It's not common, but it happens. Of course, those who choose the darkness do have one advantage. To the naked eye, they look like everyday people. Like us. Except they're not. Only Angelica and a few select Keepers can see their true form…can see their darkness."

Thea seemed taken aback at Cade's comprehensive answer, something I didn't expect. "You okay, T?"

She nodded, but she bit the corner of her lip. "You meant a few select Keepers like you and Louisa."

"Yes." He nodded. "Lou can see their reptilian form, same as me. It's off-putting, but it helps us do our job."

I needed to direct this to a more academic tack, so she didn't think about what we might face. She saw enough that morning in the botanical gardens.

"Thea, you might find this interesting," I offered. "The last time I was in the archive, I discovered the seven deadly sins were named for the vices of the seven princes of Hell, including Lucifer and Satanael."

Cade nodded. "Samael is a trip, too. He's genderless, meaning he can appear as either male or female, both or neither. He has twelve wings, and a huge set of horns, and he's hooked up with Lilith, a.k.a. Adam's first wife and primordial demoness. Not to mention he's Michael's archenemy."

"Hells Bells! Where were you two when I was failing Gods, Myths and World Religions my junior year of college?" Thea was slack-jawed, but still chuckled.

I tightened my arm in hers. "Feeling a little out of your element?"

"What gave it away?"

"The fact your laugh went up two octaves."

"Ha. Funny."

One Scythe Fits All

"Don't sweat it, sweetie. I've been doing this up close and personal for four months, and I'm still out of my element."

Cade snorted. "Try a century and a half."

We were across the street from Death Central. I looked up, and the gargoyles inclined their heads to us in acknowledgment. The movement was almost imperceptible, but Cade and I were attuned to it, so we answered in kind.

Thea looked up as well, and I expected her to shield her eyes and squint, unable to sense what we sensed, but instead she waved and then blew a kiss.

"What are you doing?" I asked.

She gave me a nonplussed look. "Saying hello, what else?"

"To whom? The pigeons?"

Her lips pushed to one side, in a who-do-you-think expression. "I'm acknowledging the gargoyles, snooty. You're not the only ones who can sense them, you know. I told you that on the beach over the summer."

"But you can't see them."

She shrugged. "Not all of them. Just the ones who have introduced themselves." A quiet smile graced her mouth. "They really are the sweetest creatures. And I thought they'd feel bristly to the touch, but they're not. They're super soft and smooth, albeit wrinkly. A little like a cross between a hairless cat and a chinchilla."

I stared at her open-mouthed. "You've petted a gargoyle? How? When?"

"I spent a lot of time at the office while you and Cade were on sabbatical after the coup attempt. I didn't know many people at Memento Mori, so I would eat my lunch on the roof. I suppose the gargoyles got used to me after a while. They're really no different than any other wild creature. Befriending them came down to a matter of trust. The rest was easy."

I looked from one to the other. "Cade, are you hearing this?"

"I hear it and I think it's terrific. I don't think enough people at Memento Mori give the gargoyles their due. So brava, Thea."

She grinned, shooting the top of the building a thumbs up. "Bix saw you on the roof with Clarence yesterday, and wanted to help, but he couldn't. Angelica doesn't encourage fraternization. He'd like to formally meet you, so I told him I'd ask."

"Bix the gargoyle wants to meet me. Why?"

The don't walk sign changed to walk and we hurried across Madison Avenue to the building. "You're an anomaly, Louisa. The gargoyles know everything that happens at Memento Mori, and in the other celestial realms, as well. They are quite the resource, and they love to gossip. We're heading to the archives, but I think we should also make a trip to the roof."

I looked at Cade and he shrugged. "It might be worth it just to see what they say, Lou. We might be able to cross reference something we find in the archive with what the gargoyles know. Scribes try their best, but they are only privy to what they are told and what they are allowed to record."

"Good." Thea pulled open a stationary door to the lobby. "We'll have to get snacks before we head to the roof. Bix and his friends like Swedish fish, but they adore sour gummy worms."

I laughed to myself. "I'll make a list. Anything else we should know?"

"Yes." She stopped with us just inside the lobby. "Don't say anything about the pigeon bones. There's quite a stockpile. It's kind of off putting, but Eddu keeps them as some sort of collection."

"Eddu?"

"Bix's brother. He's a little off, but very sweet."

"He collects bones from the pigeons he eats. I'd say that's more than a little off." I made a face. "Doesn't that stockpile attract rats?"

"Sometimes, but they don't make it very far. Our beasties are very proprietary. I was lucky they sensed my second sight, or I may have done an involuntary header off the roof the day I wandered into their domain."

I blinked a that. "Cade told me pigeon was a gargoyle favorite, but what about places like Venice, and Paris? Pigeons are a menace in those venues. Are the gargoyles there outnumbered, or don't they care for the taste of flying rat?"

"I asked Bix the same question, and he said European gargoyles are a different species, and they have different dietary needs. Asian gargoyles even more so. I guess New York is lucky. Our cutie patootie beasties keep the pigeon population from taking over."

I looked at Cade and burst out laughing. "Gargoyles, pigeons, and sour gummy worms. If this isn't the definition of surreal, then I don't know what."

The elevator took us to the archive floor. It was directly below the Department of Life Audits where Jeremiah managed the daily tedium housed within.

Cade and I had enlisted his help before the coup attempt, after Angelica dismissed our concerns. Jeremiah gave us our first lead, and I had the distinct feeling we'd be knocking on his door for help, again.

The archive floor wasn't as big as I expected. I figured it would be at least as big and well-lit as the processing center in limbo. I was wrong.

This was no bigger than a main reading room in an average public library with one major difference. Table surfaces were all flat LED screens. The large rectangular kind you see in high tech labs.

Bookshelves around the room were completely virtual, where holographic books floated from shelf to table, and were seamlessly absorbed. From there they opened in crisp, digital manuscripts.

"Wow. Talk about eBooks on steroids," Thea reacted, looking around.

I watched archivists pull documentation for patrons, helping them set reading angles for optimal use.

"This is off the chain. The Jefferson would be the talk of New York City if we had this kind of technology."

One Scythe Fits All

As cool as this holographic library seemed, it was nothing compared to the one Angelica took Cade and I to during the coup attempt—The Historia et Archivi Mortuorem.

That archive was older than dirt, and despite its elegant atmosphere, its secret, classified status gave off a solitary confinement vibe. Hell, it was housed on a covert floor, along a covert corridor, with biometrics that would make the pentagon jealous.

The documents and records housed *there* were the ones Memento Mori wanted kept quiet, so everything housed in *this* holographic library was basically gen pop.

"The sci-fi feel here is cool, but I don't think this archive has what we need, Cade." I turned in a semi-circle, noting Keepers researching everything from information on their current charges, to what was the hottest restaurant in Tribeca.

He didn't disagree, but he didn't offer an alternative, either. "What would you like to do, then?" His whisper was hurried and a little harsh. "This is an uphill climb, Lou. Forget the haystack. We don't even have a needle."

His frustration was palpable, and I got why. I had tied our hands not wanting to bring Angelica into the know. We'd never been in a place where we didn't have a plan of attack, but I had to make him understand.

"Returning the pendant to Angelica feels wrong, Cade. I'm not being petulant or proprietary. I told you, and I told Thea, something feels off. That hasn't changed since the moment Angelica called us into her office and told us about the inquest. In fact, my gut is churning even more than ever, and it's not just my nerves. Holding onto the pendant is the only ace we have right now. Until dots start connecting, I don't want to give up that edge."

He nodded, spreading a hand to what we had available. "Well, we came without a plan. So why not start here until we hit a wall?"

"I don't understand. You guys really don't have any leads?" Thea side-eyed me, but this time I truly had nothing but supposition.

"Back at the brownstone you suggested shifting our focus to bring perspective and clarity," Cade acknowledged. "Personally, I've never experienced this kind of blindness when facing conundrums, but perhaps that's what this puppeteer wants."

"See?" Thea flicked my arm. "I knew you weren't stuck. You just need an alternative route. When I have trouble with a spell, I do this, too, except my brain detours usually involve food." She looked from me to Cade and back again. "So, do you have something or someone in mind?"

Cade and I answered together. "Charlotte."

Chapter Fourteen

"WHO'S CHARLOTTE?" Thea asked. "Is she a Keeper?"

"She's a ghost currently haunting my back yard." I explained what I witnessed during the spirit dive, and the more I talked, the more Thea's face furrowed into a scowl.

"Please tell me that creep died. That he didn't pass go, didn't collect two hundred dollars, and went straight to jail by way of the darkness."

Cade looked at the LED tables and then back again. "That sounds like a good starting point. Everything we need is literally at our fingertips."

We grabbed the first available table, and Cade activated the screen. "Lou, can you remember Charlotte's full name? I remember it was an Irish surname, but I can't recall what."

"Fitzgerald…and her husband was Dan, or Danny. I don't know if that was short for Daniel or Dannel or some other iteration."

Cade worked the screen, tapping the information into the database. "We have enough to go one to start."

He pressed enter, and the screen immediately flashed with Charlotte's full name and the book stats that housed her file.

"It's asking if we want to see her file or not."

"Of course, we want to see her file," I answered quickly. "How else can we get her death date and life particulars?"

Thea craned over Cade's arm, watching the screen flash page after page. "We could search census documents for the same information. If she died in the United States in the last century it shouldn't be hard to find."

A book floated toward us with the words Mid-Atlantic States 1970 glowing on its spine. It rested on the LED screen and once it connected to the main server, disappeared in a gleam and a blip.

"You are totally getting your *Star Wars* on right now, aren't you?" Thea teased, knowing she was one hundred percent right.

"Laugh it up, Fuzzball."

Cade promised he'd watch all twelve movies in the saga over our next marathon, plus the bridge movies and then the *Mandalorian*.

"And we're in." Cade touched the book with Charlotte's particulars, and her hologram rose from the pertinent page.

She looked older. Sadder. When I checked her stats, her age at death read forty-five years, ten months, two days, five hours, three minutes, and twelve seconds.

One Scythe Fits All

"Is it always that accurate?" Thea asked.

Cade nodded, scrolling for more statistics. "That's the one thing about the universe you can count on. Accuracy down to the second. It's a necessary evil. With so many births and deaths, timestamps are a foolproof way to keep order."

I looked at the hologram again. Her expression was more than simple sadness or even clinical depression. She looked lost. I reached over Cade's arm and touched a finger to the image on the digital page used to generate the hologram. I touched the part of her chest where the reaper had damaged her soul.

The hologram flashed, and the image changed to a three dimensional silhouette. At the center of her chest was a vertical scar. Records showed a cardio-thoracic incident, but I knew that was a lie.

The records were wrong, which told me the scribe charged with documenting Charlotte's death was given false information. That scar wasn't made by human hands.

I removed my finger, my mind racing with what else might be false. "Cade, is there an entry as to cause of death?"

He scrolled back to her death stamp, and then forward again before stopping. "That's odd. There's no mention of how Charlotte died. Her death stamp is clearly noted, and directly after is where cause of death should be listed."

"Do you guys know how she died?" Thea questioned. "Does anything else not jive with what you know?"

I shared a look with Cade. "A couple of things don't add up, but sometimes memory is skewed during a spirit dive. We'll have to cross-reference this record with any others in the archive."

"On it." Cade already typed away, setting the first book aside and searching for other records. "I'll see if I can narrow down mid-Atlantic states to something more like an address."

Thea took a chair opposite Cade, already typing in a question for the database. "I want to give this floating library a shot. Let's search something common and well documented, like the Angel of Death and her sister."

"Why?" I asked. "Whatever records you find won't bring anything pertinent onto Charlotte's case. Besides, I doubt there's anything listed in this reserve that isn't public relations or spin. Basically, Wikipedia and IMDb for celestials."

She shrugged, still typing. "So, it's Google on steroids. Big whoop."

Was Thea's curious cat impression for my sake? I know she saw my expression when I pulled up the second hologram.

"Bingo!" She leaned in, reading the screen as it scrolled in real time. "This is good. Really good."

"What?"

"I'm paraphrasing here, but says there used to be thirteen archangels, including both Morana and Angelica. Angelica's celestial name is Azrael, the Archangel of Death."

"I knew that already. She told me the first day I met her."

"Yeah, but this says Morana used to be the Archangel of Tears, and that she was one of the angels who defied the universal divine along with the other fallen angels who followed Lucifer in his rebellion.

One Scythe Fits All

According to this, Angelica pleaded with some guy called Metatron to intercede on behalf of her sister."

"Metatron? He sounds like a transformer."

Cade looked up from his search. "It's a weird name, but he's the one to see if you want anything done. He and his twin, Sandalphon. They are the intercessors."

"They're both weird names."

"Yup. That's why they go by M.T. and Sandy." Cade stopped on a particular page. "I think I have something. This record mentions Charlotte dying of core withering. That's code for a dying soul. It withers in place and causes a myriad of issues that usually end in suicide."

Thea blew out a breath out. "That poor woman."

"She didn't deserve what happened to her, and that's why we're here. Cade and I promised we'd get to the bottom of why she was targeted."

"I'll see if I can narrow this further, but it says she lived on Long Island when she died."

Thea went back to her own scrolling, chewing on her left thumbnail. "So, Morana wasn't forgiven. She was cast down with the rest until Michael intervened. He had her assigned as The Grim. Still a minion of the darkness, but she'd be the equal and opposite of her sister, with full access to Angelica and the human realm as a whole."

She looked up from the screen. "If we can be forgiven, why not angels? It doesn't seem fair. All we need to do is a sincere mia culpa, maybe say a few rosaries if that's your gig, but relatively easy peasy. For witchy women like me, it's even easier. As long as it harm none, do as ye will. The rule of three is karma in action. Whatever harm you do is returned to you three fold."

"In other words, don't be an asshole. Or do unto others as you would have them do unto you."

She nodded. "The Golden Rule. It belongs to all yet owned by none. The original universal."

"Angels can't be shown to be guilty of pride," Cade confided. "It all goes back to Lucifer's famous last words. 'Better to reign in Hell, than serve in Heaven.' Still, that's not the whole story. Michael intervened for Morana because she was his main squeeze."

Thea pressed her lips together not to laugh. "His what?"

"His sweetheart. Isn't that the slang for who one is keeping company with?"

I looked up from looking over Thea's shoulder. "Not since the 1970s."

"Fine. Morana was his lover. I'm telling you. The man is a horndog. He felt guilty because he broke off their relationship, which is why she fell in with Lucifer and his crowd. Morana never wanted to rebel against Heaven. She got swept up."

My guilty pleasure was reality television, and *this* was the O.G. of all trainwrecks. "Wait. I thought that was from John Milton's *Paradise Lost*."

"And who do you think acted as Milton's muse?" Cade posed. "Whispering in his ear as he wrote?"

Thea didn't take her eyes from the screen. "The great deceiver, a.k.a. Satanael."

"No way."

Cade nodded. "It happens more than you know.

"Wow. Makes sense. With all the crap cinema and cheesy, unnecessary reboots these days, someone better fire up the altar under the Hollywood sign for whispered inspiration."

Cade's eyes were a definite warning I had come too close to some sort of line. "I was joking!"

"Please don't. It's one thing to look up dirt on Morana, but don't invoke the darkness, even in jest. It never bodes well."

Thea was nodding as well. "It's like we witches say. Don't call it to you."

"Bingo!" Cade pointed to a page on the LED screen, and then moved his in a sweeping motion to lift the page in holographic form. There it was in glowing letters.

Charlotte Madigan Fitzgerald
Died: Forty-five years, ten months, two days, five hours, three minutes, and twelve seconds.
*Death: By her own hand. *See withering.*
Journey status: Tethered and incomplete.

Seeing it there in bright digital form was too stark. Too cut and dried. Nothing about her story or what she suffered.

"It's right there in the records for all to see. Core withering. You said that's code for an incomplete soul. You'd think that would raise a red flag."

Thea nodded. "Or at least prompt someone to ask the obvious question. Did Charlotte sell her soul? If she did, then her inner withering is justified. BUT she didn't. She was a victim, and no one paid attention."

All the levity strides we made to break the tension disappeared. This sucked. For Charlotte, and for however many more souls were left languishing from inattention. "Do we have an address at time of death?" I asked, suddenly very tired.

Cade nodded. "I've written it down."

"Good. We need to cross check that address to see if it's the same street where she was neighbors with Stan."

He folded the note with Charlotte's address and handed it to me before closing the files and the holograms.

"I think we should head home," Thea suggested. "I've got my laptop. We can get comfy and order in food and then hit the internet to look for that creeper."

"Thea's right. You need a break, Lou. I know you always follow your gut, and mine is telling me that Stan isn't dead. I tried to cast a wide net based on Charlotte's address, but no one with the name Stan came up in the search. Either Charlotte moved away from the street where she was neighbors with that absolute horror of a human being, or he's not dead."

"His wife's name was Shirley. Poor woman," I added.

Cade got up from his seat to slip his arms around my shoulders. "We can always ask Charlotte. Not another spirit dive, but ask her, nonetheless. I know she can't speak to us, but maybe we can use something else."

He slid his eyes to Thea, who nodded. "I have just the thing. We just need to stop at my shop on the way downtown."

I was a woman on a mission at this point. The sadness that exhausted me in the archive library was gone, and a new fire burned in my belly.

Taking the front stairs two at a time, I unlocked both the front and vestibule doors, leaving them wide open for Cade and Thea bringing up the rear.

The house was dark, and I stalked straight for the kitchen, turning on every light as I passed. It wasn't necessary, but I didn't care. It was symbolic. I would

157

One Scythe Fits All

leave no corner unlit, no place lightless to help Charlotte and hopefully help myself in the process.

Thea puffed in behind Cade, shooting me daggers for making her hustle. "Girl, do you want this curvy body to collapse? I told you. I was built for comfort. Not speed."

"Last I heard, you said your curves were built for bouncing, and if memory serves it was in reference to a certain angel named Michael."

Cade's head jerked around at that. "I am going to pretend I didn't hear that."

"Why?" Thea asked, putting her large duffle bag on one of the counter stools. "You think you're the only hottie celestial?"

"That's not what I... I mean, no...of course not... Michael is...I mean..."

"Easy lover," Thea teased. "Or you'll give yourself a cramp."

Cade sat at the counter with a muffled grumble.

"Michael is what, Cade?" I put my hand on the middle of his back, rubbing tiny circles with my fingers. "You wouldn't have tripped over your own tongue if it wasn't important. I know how much you care about my friend."

"Tripped?" Thea raised both brows. "He stuttered worse than Elvis."

Cade shot Thea a look. "Elvis didn't stutter."

"Oh yes he did. He had help, but why else do you think he spoke so slowly? Now, why did my appreciation of Michael's very endowed person send you into fits?"

"Because Michael is a player, to use the modern vernacular. He's very sure of himself when it comes to human females. You think that dance scene with John Travolta in the movie *Michael* was just poetic license?"

I couldn't help a little snorty giggle. "You mean he really smells like cookies? I must've missed that when he showed up at the botanical gardens."

Cade shrugged out from under my hand. "Forget it. Thea can drool over that winged erection all she wants."

I bit my tongue until I tasted blood, but Thea cackled like the witch from the *Wizard of Oz*.

"Now that's a visual I will keep!"

Hmph.

"Aw, Cade, don't be like that," I tried. "Your description was funny as hell, and I appreciate you trying to protect Thea."

He shook his head, but a tiny grin tickled the corner of his mouth.

"As do I," Thea admitted. "Though I am a grown woman and a *witch*, so I could make that flying erection lose altitude very quickly if needs be."

That turned Cade's itch of a smirk into a full grin. "Something I'd pay to watch." He squinched his eyes closed. "Yep. Heard it. Not good. Did not mean that literally. I do NOT want to see Michael's peen."

Thea and I both roared at that, and Cade went three shades of red. "Maybe we should get to whatever Thea had in mind to scry for Charlotte's attacker."

Wiping my eyes with my cuff, I went to the fridge to grab a chilled bottle of wine and then the cupboard for three glasses.

"We have tons of leftover Chinese in the fridge if anyone's hungry. If not we can order pizza. I'm kind of in the mood for Sicilian, then again, I don't want to stop what we're doing to answer the door."

One Scythe Fits All

"Then leftovers it is." Cade took the wine and the glasses from me, and I grabbed the white folded cartons from the refrigerator to put in the microwave.

Thea opened her duffle and pulled out a very familiar wooden rectangle, and I stopped with my hand on the microwave door. "You did not just bring a Ouija board into this house."

She looked at me with the spirit board halfway to the table. "I did, why?"

"This house is already surrounded by ghosts in various and sundry forms. That board opens portals. I don't need other specters and entities squatting, especially not INSIDE."

The small side grin on Thea's face irked, as if I said something stupid. "Thea, I'm serious. Even you said Ouija boards are unsafe."

"Unsafe in the hands of amateurs! Of people playing at being witches. I know what I'm doing, Louisa. I would never endanger your space or leave any of us open to danger. Besides, we won't be engaging that way. I am not calling to spirits out in the ether. Charlotte is already here. We're just using the board for the alphabet."

I blinked at her for a moment. "No portal."

"No, ma'am."

"Are you casting a protective circle?"

"If it'll make you feel better, sure. Why not?"

I spared a look for Cade who wasn't saying a word. He just poured the wine, but I noted he poured my glass way above problem sized.

"Okay. I'll invite Charlotte into the kitchen."

Thea shrugged, putting the Ouija board on the kitchen counter with its planchette. "If you'd rather do this outside, we can, but I warded this house within an inch of its bricks imploding. Nothing is getting through that we don't allow."

I nodded again, and then went to the back door. I opened it to find four ghosts sitting around my café set and another few on the small patio swing. It looked so much like a scene from Disney's Haunted Mansion ride I was taken aback for a moment.

"Charlotte?" I called into the gloom. The translucent woman floated across the grass from the fence, acknowledging me with a nod when she got to the small flagstone patio.

"I need you to come inside." The ghost hung back for a moment, but then edged closer. "It's okay, Charlotte. We need your help to clarify some of our research. Not another spirit dive, so don't worry. We think we may have another way you can communicate with us."

Her silvery gray face seemed relieved, and though ghosts don't actually breathe, she exhaled anyway before floating past me into the kitchen.

Whether they were truly interested or just nosy, the other ghosts craned to see into the kitchen, but I shut that down. "I will help each of you in your own time. I know waiting sucks, but I've been to limbo. You do not want to do your waiting there. Trust me. It's boring."

There was a general muttering hum, so I took that as a positive. I could've threatened them with expulsion, but after seeing that hope desert they call a processing center, I didn't have the heart. Besides, nothing was going to spoil my high. It was time to play let's find a creep.

Chapter Fifteen

I TOOK CADE'S FOLDED PIECE OF PAPER from my pocket and smoothed it on the kitchen counter.

Thea had her laptop fired up and ready. We three were on a mission for one soul, but hoping our efforts bore fruit for the bigger questions.

"Charlotte," I began awkwardly knowing Thea couldn't see the ghost. "You know Cade, and this is my friend Thea. She came up with the idea to use the spirit board to communicate."

The ghost actually frowned, and then retreated a few steps toward the back door. Could spirits sense the inherent danger in tapping on the unknown?

"We're not playing with portals, Charlotte. I promise. We just want you to move the planchette to spell out answers to our questions."

Lifting her hand, she went to touch the heart-shaped coaster, but it passed straight through the physical item.

"I was afraid of that," Cade replied. "It was a good idea, but I think we may have to connect with Charlotte the way we know best."

Charlotte's entire being seemed to deflate. I had said no spirit dive and no portals. We had to think of something else.

"What if Charlotte touched one of us?" I asked. "The night we did her spirit dive, I held her tether item in my hand. If I can do that, maybe that button could provide a connection."

Thea perked up at that. "Do you still have the button?"

Charlotte opened her hand. The small gold button with the embossed anchor design sat at the center of her palm.

"Charlotte, do you remember dropping your tether item from your hand before Cade and I initiated your spirit dive?" I asked, hoping it wasn't just a one off.

The ghost nodded and then lifted her hand, same as she did the night I merged my mind with her memories. Turning her palm over, she let the tether item tumble from her palm. I held my breath until I heard the soft plink on the kitchen floor.

"Shut the front door!" Thea stood from her highbacked stool. She shivered, doing a heebie jeebies wiggle. "Give a girl a heads up next time!"

"Wait, you felt that?" I asked, bending to retrieve the button from where it bounced under a chair.

"Hells yes. Are you saying you didn't?"

Cade shook his head the same as me.

"The air shifted. Silken, yet creepy and hairy. Like walking through a thick spider web." She shivered again. "Fat Indiana Jones Temple of Doom spider webs.

"I didn't feel a thing," I replied, nonplussed. "Not a single ripple let alone the heebie jeebies."

"Forget the heebie jeebies, Lou. Do you have the button?" Cade asked, getting us back on track.

I opened my hand the same as the ghost had, and there it was, complete with the blue threads from where Charlotte ripped it from Stan's jacket.

"How did that button sift from the ethereal into the physical plane?" Thea stared at it in my hand, but she didn't move to touch it.

"I have no idea. Tether items are only in the physical plane when a spirit box is in use. Ghost boxes are proprietary to Memento Mori and only used by Keepers. It's very unusual for a ghost to sift physical items.

Cade took the button from me, running his internal fraud-o-meter on it again. "There's nothing usual about anything we've encountered this week, so I suggest we lower our expectations."

He handed the button back to me. "It's clean."

"Forget lowered expectations," I replied. "Maybe no expectations would be best."

Thea sat on her stool again, scraping it closer to the kitchen counter. "Or expect the worst and hope for the best."

"Are we done with greeting card sayings?" Cade looked at us again. "If you haven't noticed, Charlotte's translucence is fading. I suspect it has something to do her tether being in the physical plane. The longer it's here, the more it drains her energy."

I hadn't noticed, and I felt awful. I put the button on the planchette, and then nodded to the ghost. "I'm sorry, honey. Let's begin."

She reached her fingers toward the tether item, and it hummed. "So far, so good." I encouraged. "Now see if you can move the planchette with it."

The ghost's hand went through the heart-shaped coaster again, but it pushed the button from the coaster's flat top onto the board.

"Okay. Trial and error, take two." I nodded. "Just the button this time."

Thea took the planchette off the board, and like magic, Charlotte moved the button around with ease.

"Woot!" I clapped, grinning like I won the lottery. "Good for you, girl!"

Charlotte's ethereal smile lit up her face and warmed the whole kitchen.

Cade showed her the paper with the address listed from the archive at Memento Mori. "Was this your address?"

She nodded.

"Did you live here when you were neighbors with Stan?"

She shook her head no, and her hand trembled hovering above the button on the Ouija board. "It's okay, honey. He can't hurt you anymore."

I wanted to promise the evil creep had a world of hurt waiting for him, but I didn't want to upset her further."

"Do you remember that address, Charlotte?" Cade's voice was gentle. He didn't want to push her either. "We really need it so we can find out what happened to Stan. If he's alive or dead."

Her pale shimmering face hardened, and she pushed the button around the board like a wild woman. Thea scribbled the letters down, writing as quickly as Charlotte spelled out her message.

One Scythe Fits All

"What did she say?" I asked, trying to read Thea's writing upside down.

"She said, 'I hope the bastard is rotting in Hell.'"

I wanted to high five the ghost, but my hand would've passed right through hers. "If Stan has passed on, I can almost guarantee you he is in the darkness. If he's still alive, then he has no idea what awaits him."

Having only the Judeo-Christian construct to go by, I imagined all sorts of very painful yet satisfying tortures awaiting that man. Cade would fill me in later on what really waited in the darkness, like icy emptiness so cold it burned. Or so I hoped.

"If you give us your address and the timeframe he was your neighbor, we will let you know if he's cosmic compost or not." Cade seemed as stoked as me to find out if karma took a large bite out of Stan's butt.

Charlotte moved the button around the board, concentrating so hard her tongue peeked out of the corner of her mouth.

Thea stood from her stool with the pad and pen in her hand, scribbling letters one at a time.

"Got it." She gestured with the spiral pad, but Charlotte raised one greyish hand, stopping Thea from resuming her seat.

"More?" she asked the ghost, and Charlotte nodded.

The button moved over six final letters. She had given us Stan's last name. Murphy.

I wanted to hug her shimmery form so hard, but the only way to do that would be to do another spirit dive, and neither of us had the strength for that.

"You did it, Charlotte. You. Did. It."

With the brightest grin, she opened her palm to show us the button was back in her grasp before she disappeared through my back door into the yard.

I still had no idea how or why that small, innate object had traversed planes of existence. Maybe it had to do with how it came to tether Charlotte. That it wasn't tied to her last moments, but instead, the moments that changed the trajectory of her life. Or maybe it had to do with Stan and whether or not he was still alive. It was another mystery added to the already growing pile.

"How amazing was that!" Thea did another little dance, her jiggly bits bobbling under her boho style dress. "It was a total trip watching that button move across the spirit board. I totally get why paranormal investigators cream in their pants when ghosts respond. I'm going to buy mt own equipment so I can communicate next time."

"Why?" I asked. "You did great on your own."

Thea wrinkled her nose, cocking her head. "I wanted to talk to Charlotte. See her like you two. Maybe I'll buy a ghost box. Not a transport like Keepers use. I mean a Frank's Box so I can hear and speak to the other side."

"It doesn't work that way, Thea," Cade replied. "With a Frank's Box, spirits talk *through* you, not to you. Plus, it requires sensory deprivation in order to work."

She sucked her teeth. "I'll figure out something. If I'm going to be part of this team, I want all the bells and whistles."

"You could always ask Angelica to make you a Keeper," Cade suggested. "Then you'd have access to all kinds of spirits."

Her eyes lit for a moment, but then she shook her head. "I'm a witch. I'm guessing that's counterintuitive to the process."

One Scythe Fits All

"Not necessarily," I offered. "I'm a recovering Catholic who hadn't stepped inside a church for decades. I don't think it matters to the universal divine."

She considered again, taking one of the wine glasses Cade freshened for us. "When this is over and you're cleared of all charges, I'll think about it."

Putting her wine glass down, she stowed the Ouija board back in her duffle bag and then put the duffle on the floor by her chair.

"First things first." Thea woke her laptop from sleep mode. "Now that we have Stan the Creeper Man's name, we can check for a death certificate on any of the ancestry sites. If nothing comes up, then we check census records, real estate transactions, etc."

I got my laptop as well, plugging it in beside Thea's to work in tandem. "While you check that, I'll do a Google search for his name. If one comes up with his address, I can do a deeper dive using people finder."

Cade transferred the leftover Chinese food into serving dishes and popped the first in the microwave. "Considering the timeframe, I think it's a stretch we'll find Stan still alive. Even if he was a few years younger than Charlotte, he'd be extremely old."

"Don't be negative," Thea clicked away at her keyboard. "The man was warped enough to attract the darkness. That's the equivalent of enough piss and vinegar to preserve a cow."

I paused with my hand on my mouse scanning the page on my screen. "I think Cade might be right. Or about to be anyway."

They both got up to peer over my shoulder from either side. Stan wasn't dead, but he was circling the drain.

"He's been in jail this whole time." I read the newspaper article again. "He got off with a boys-will-be-boys slap on the wrist for what he did to Charlotte, but karma took the bite out of his butt I hoped for. I can't wait to tell Charlotte."

I looked at Thea. "Is there a way to see his police record? It's Long Island, NY, so arrests and conviction records should be a matter of public record, right?"

She nodded, typing again. "It's a searchable database. Thankfully we have his full name otherwise it would be a stretch. Let's hope none of his records were sealed or expunged."

It didn't take long for Thea to find the pertinent documents. She turned her screen around.

"Christ! He's got a rap sheet longer than my arm." Cade leaned in reading as Thea scrolled. "Sexual assault. Rape. Battery. Domestic abuse. He was an equal opportunity bully and misogynist."

I made a face. "He was worse than that, Cade. He was a predator."

Thea stopped at the last entry. "He was last held at Beechwood Psychiatric Prison in central New York. I've heard about that place. It's high security, so it's got a medical wing.

Cade moved to my laptop, logging out of Google and into the Keeper portal for Memento Mori.

"What are you looking for?" I asked, looking over his shoulder now.

"This," he said, tapping the screen. "I had a hunch, so I figured I'd check. Stan's not doing well. He's already got a Keeper assigned, which isn't surprising considering his dark nature. It's company practice to make sure souls slotted for darkness aren't snatched. There's always the chance they could be reconstituted as reapers instead of reaping the consequences for what they sowed in life."

He scrolled pages, stopping again to point at the screen. "Just as I thought. Our guy was moved to the jail's medical facility for terminal cancer. He was given six months to live." He looked at me. "That was five months ago, and the final note at the bottom of the Keeper's record was he was comatose."

"We need to get in there, Cade. If he's in a coma, I can pretend to be someone…next of kin…a hospice worker…anything, so long and I can make skin-to-skin contact. Considering his state, holding his hand won't look out of place. I can do a mind meld with him the same way I did with Rose."

He got up, closing the laptop's lid. "No. You almost didn't come out of that one."

"I know, so I'll need you to ground me. We need to see if there's a dark trace buried somewhere inside that creep's mind before he croaks. Like you said, with everything this man has done in his life, there is no salvation waiting at the end of his audit, even if his Keeper can prove compulsion.

"I saw what happened. I watched the darkness leave him the same night Charlotte's soul was fractured. He was compelled in that instance only. What he did and the lives he shattered after that were all him and only him."

He leaned against the kitchen sink, the food on the counter untouched by us all. "I don't know, Lou. I don't like it. Doing a mind meld with someone this evil, this corrupted is dangerous. I have lightyears more experience than you, and I wouldn't want to touch his warped psyche."

"What if you did the mind meld together?" Thea posed. "I could do a grounding spell beforehand. I could even bind you both to each other, doubly insuring your protection."

I looked at Cade, and I didn't need to ask. He was not happy about it, but Thea's protection and insurance made it palatable.

Lifting my wine glass, I held it up in concurrence. "Deal?"

He nodded slowly, still not happy. "Deal, but only if Thea comes up with one more protection protocol. Three is a magical number, right? Three of us. Three spells…" he paused. "Three days."

"Three days?" I questioned. "Why?"

Thea lifted her glass as well. "Because that's how long it will take for us to get permission to visit our creeper." She inclined her head. "Well done, dude. Three times three times three. Plus, at that point it will be a new moon. Hecate's moon. The goddess of boundaries, transitions, crossroads, magic, necromancy, and ghosts. It's perfect."

We toasted our plan of attack, but Cade hung back, quiet. We had three days to strategize, and to help Thea gather the ingredients she needed for her spell craft.

I still wasn't willing to bring Angelica into this until we had something concrete to merit her attention. The celestial set was noise blind. It wasn't surprising. Not with millennia behind them, and millennia ahead. They didn't sweat the small stuff. At the same time the devil was in the details, and those details were often so under the radar they were easy to miss.

How else would Angelica and Morana's own brother, who'd already been demoted to Watcher angel, plan and execute a coup against them both?

One Scythe Fits All

That small nudgy twist gripped my stomach, the same way it had at every untoward turn of events these past four months. Only now that twist in my gut was stronger than ever. Something was off. I didn't have to convince Cade. He knew it, too. So did Thea. The hard nut was Angie.

Hard or not, I had to find evidence and present it to her in a way that would make her sit up at her desk and take notice. Her, Morana, and Michael…and whoever lurked in the shadowed darkness pulling the strings.

"I think I'm going to head home." Thea stretched, yawning. "The little grey cells are fried. Heady merlot, notwithstanding. Besides, I'm starving, yet the idea of leftover Chinese food doesn't seem that appealing anymore."

I chuckled, nodding. "Not when it's been sitting on the counter for two hours." I glanced at the clock. It was nearly midnight. Witching hour.

"Thea, why don't you stay the night? It's so late, plus you've got clothes and toiletries already stowed in the guest room. Hell, that room is practically *your* room."

Cade agreed. "Lou's right. Stay. We can discuss our plans more over pancakes in the morning."

"That depends." She wore an expression I'd know anywhere.

"Banana or chocolate chip?" he guessed.

"Nope. Blueberry with real bacon on the side." She got up from her highbacked stool to smooth her dress over her hips. "Curves built for comfort need the right kind of care."

With a wink, Cade opened the fridge and pulled out two pints of ripe, plump blueberries the size of his thumb pad. "Way ahead of you, T."

"I knew I liked you." She yawned again. "Fresh ground coffee, too. The spells I have planned require me firing on all cylinders."

She walked out of the kitchen with a tired wave, leaving her laptop on the counter. Cade put the blueberries back in the refrigerator and then leaned on the sink again.

"What about you?" he asked. "What do you want to help you fire on all cylinders?"

I got up and walked into his arms. "Remember what you said about not taking my comment on everlasting batteries for my adult toys too seriously?"

A sexy, crooked grin slipped across his lips. "I remember."

"Why don't we give those batteries a run for their money?"

He laughed, throwing me over his shoulder before heading to the stairs. "You're wish is my command, Energizer Bunny."

Chapter Sixteen

WE SAT IN AN EMPTY WAITING room across from admitting. The registration desk was at the center, with double doors leading to the ambulance bay on the left, and triage on the right.

This part of the hospital was admitting, a relatives room, and emergency department all rolled into one.

From here, it looked no different than any hospital waiting room. Innocuous plants, molded plastic chairs and synthetic couches separated by small rectangular tables, and a corner, wall-mounted television displaying The Weather Channel in closed captions. A typical hospital, except for the armed security guards and metal detectors.

Thea must've pulled out all spell casting stops because we had three passes into the facility.

Beechwood was a prison hospital, with a stress on the word prison. The complex housed violent criminals of all kinds, including serial sex offenders like Stanley Murphy.

We passed through an initial security check when we arrived. I.D.s and a walk through the metal detector at the door. However, before we entered the hospital's interior domain, we'd have to go through another series of checks including a pat down.

Getting in to see Stan so I could wade through his warped mind wasn't a picnic, but we had no choice. We'd yet to lay eyes on the man, and already my stomach churned. Not from a gut warning. There was no exterior threat sending red flags, just a bad taste in my mouth at what I might witness inside his head.

"What's wrong?" Cade asked, keeping his voice low. "You look a little like you want to throw up."

"I wish this was done and dusted already. That's all."

He put his arm around my shoulders. "You're not doing this alone, and if it comes down to hospital rules allowing only one person in at a time, I'll take the lead on this dive."

"But..."

"No arguments, Lou." Cade was as adamant as he was last night. "We agreed already. You are not doing this alone."

Thea was in complete agreement and didn't waste a minute taking Cade's side. "Girl, I'm usually all in when it comes to calling on the divine feminine, but this case requires more than raw determination. Cade has more experience than you. Not better, just more. None of us considered the possibility the prison might only allow one visitor at a time. We need to roll with it, accordingly."

"Why don't we cross that bridge when we get there," I replied, knowing full well we were already there.

"Louisa, the man inside this facility is not the same man you saw in Charlotte's memories." I went to argue, but she stopped me cold. "The man you witnessed was under compulsion, but still had hold of his inherent humanity. The man we're about to see forfeited that humanity the moment he gave in to his base nature. The warped evil that allowed him to hurt all those young girls. You absolutely cannot enter that man's psyche alone. It's simply not safe."

I was torn. I shouldn't be, but I was, despite knowing both Cade and Thea were most likely correct.

"Lou, I understand how connected you feel to Charlotte. To the promises we made. Your loyalty and determination are some of things I love about you."

I smirked for a moment. "There's a *but* in there somewhere."

"There is no *but* in this scenario." A soft non-judgmental smile met my uncertain gaze. "You are more than capable of handling a difficult mind meld. That's not the issue. This case isn't difficult. It's dangerous. I've been a Keeper much longer than you, and I've seen what can happen when a damaged psyche overpowers an open mind during a merge. Those occurrences happened when the psyche in question belonged to the dead. Stan Murphy is very much alive inside his comatose state. Alive and starved for connection. The kind of connection that feeds his twisted need to control and terrorize."

A loud buzzer sounded and the locked reinforced door to the inner facility opened. A male nurse who looked as though he could double as a bouncer, or a Hells Angel, stood outside the closed door holding a clipboard.

"Louisa Jericho, Cade Praestes, and Thea Morgan." He read off our names roll call style despite the fact we were the only visitors in the waiting area.

"That's us," I replied, standing first, and then motioning for Cade and Thea to do the same. If we approached together, he might let us in together.

His scrutinizing gaze reminded me of Angelica's unblinking stare, and I wondered for half a second if he could be celestial, or even a reaper, but as I had no physical reaction to him or anyone else, no. It was most likely just his job.

"You're here to see Stan Murphy." The man paused after his statement, as if waiting for verbal confirmation though our reasons for visiting were on the form in front of him.

I was here to do the dirty work. Thea had made the arrangements granting visitation, so she could run interference. Especially since I didn't trust myself not to overshare.

One Scythe Fits All

"Stan is our great grandfather. I supplied the necessary familial records when I petitioned the prison for visitation."

The burly guard gave the paperwork a cursory glance. "Murphy was moved here from the cells a month ago, but records show no one has visited him since his sentencing twenty-four years ago." His eyebrow and his scam antennae were up.

Thea went to answer, but Cade got there first. "While we appreciate your due diligence, Officer, it casts aspersions on my wife and her cousin for wanting to visit a man their family hid from them for most of their lives." Cade paused, and I knew he worked some Keeper guru trick I'd yet to learn.

"You do know why gramps is incarcerated, right?" the man asked.

Thea straightened her shoulders. "Of course. His actions are a stain on humanity, but no one should die alone. He's circling the drain, but rest assured we're here for ourselves, not for him."

That, and whatever hoodoo Cade cast, did the trick. He swiped his card through the security metrics and the heavy door buzzed open.

"Normally, we only allow one visitor at a time, but as he's not long for this world, I'll make the exception. You've got fifteen minutes."

That was it. The guard didn't say another word as he led us toward Stan's hospital room.

The ward wasn't very large, considering the size of the prison facility it adjoined. My nostrils burned with the combined scent of antiseptic and detergent, while apathy seemed to be the aura of the day. I expected nurses and security staff buzzing around the hallways, but the ward was disturbingly quiet.

Locked doors lined either side of the corridor, with single reinforced glass panes at their center. "This is a hospital. Why are all the doors locked?" I queried. "What if someone codes?"

"This isn't Mount Sinai, lady. It's a prison hospital. We're understaffed, we're underpaid, and under concerned. The doors stay locked for our safety as well as theirs."

He stopped in front of the last door at the end of the main corridor. The name on the taped strip read, "Murphy, Stan."

With another swipe of his I.D. card, the door snicked open same as the one leading into the ward. "The door stays open during visitation. If I see the door shut, you're out." He eyed us all. "Understood?"

"Loud and clear, Officer," I replied. "Thank you."

"Good. Fifteen minutes." With a curt nod, he left us to it.

Cade went into the room ahead of me and Thea. I don't know what I expected, but it wasn't what we found in that bed.

The man was skeletal. Thinner than anything I'd seen short of documentaries on WW2. He had a feeding tube up his nose, and EKG leads hooked to his chest. The monitor beside his bed beeped in slow registering sounds letting the staff know he was still alive.

One Scythe Fits All

Cade lifted the man's chart from the slot on the end of his bed and flipped through the pages, stopping at a telltale yellow sheet.

"He has a DNR order in place," he said, showing us the yellow page on the clipboard.

"And?" I replied.

"It means if his heartrate increases during the mind merge, the machine will register the irregularity and alert the nurses' station."

Thea glanced at the door and then took three crystals from her purse along with a rolled piece of snakeskin leather and a bit of wax paper with bright purple petals wrapped inside.

"What are you doing?" I whispered, watching her place two of the crystals on either side of the door inside the room.

"I'm a witch doing witchy things, now shush so I can concentrate. If I touch this monkshood, it's me who'll need the crash cart 'cause I'll be the one coding."

"Oh my God! Thea, stop!"

She waved me away. "The crystals are amaranth. They're for illusion. The white quartz augments their power, and the monkshood inside snakeskin brings the final touch. Those pesky machines can beep all they want. The nurses will see and hear nothing out of the ordinary. I can't stop time, so tick tock. Get going or the sands will run out before we do what we came to do."

I stood for another moment watching her, completely floored at her foresight.

"Louisa!" She snapped her fingers. "GO."

Cade signaled for us to flank the same side of the bed. I figured we'd tag team and each take one of Stan's papery hands, but Cade wanted to stay close. Both physically and psychically.

"Ready?" he asked. "I'm taking point. You can still guide where you need, but I will be the one he senses and sees most. It's safer that way."

Fear was the enemy. Predators like Stan fed on fear. Lapping at its metallic tang to slake their addiction.

I closed my eyes after Cade's lids dropped. I hadn't ridden shotgun on a mind merge ever. From my first days as a Keeper, I had the ability to see into a soul's past and find the exact moment their essence tethered itself to an earthly object. The more complex the bond, the better.

Ten seconds passed and I disconnected from reality. Stan's papery skin was cold and dry to the touch. I almost laughed at the irony. The man was coldhearted snake in life, so it fit.

"Lou, can you sense me?" Cade's voice feathered across my mind, and I had a moment of déjà vu. Except this time, he was in the driver's seat.

"Yes."

"Good. Stay under his radar. Do not react no matter what we witness."

A familiar crackle skittered along my flesh. Cade was in the lead, so I trusted the feeling and him to let it take us where we needed to go.

As always, the crackle was pure energy, even in the backseat. Cade held Stan's hand, and I had the creeper's wrist. Live current spread from there up my arm to my throat. The pulsing energy tightened around my heart and lungs as if milking the lifeforce from my body.

The feeling was alien and it was only Cade's calming presence that stopped me from breaking the connection.

I sensed his concern, but it felt distant. He was locked in, and it was go time. My blood iced, threatening to splinter in my veins. I held on, repeating the same words in a mantra. Fear is not your friend. Fear is NOT your friend.

I slowed my breathing in time with Cade's, and the slash of panic faded as quickly as it tried to grab hold. Was this normal for a Keeper second? I had done a mind merge with Rose while she was alive, and it was nothing like this. Was that because I was driving the process, then? Or was this panic-laced chill a direct response to the warped mind we breached?

The crackling heightened to full-on body buzz and my limbs numbed. At least that felt familiar, as did the floaty emptiness that always preceded the advent of memory.

Images formed slowly, as expected. Fragmented and jagged. Cade took control, fast-forwarding through the soft recollections Stan's brain padded around his true nature.

The man was a consummate manipulator. A true predator than knew how to play each victim until it was too late to save themselves.

I held my breath as Cade did his best to reject layer upon layer of vice and violence. My insides knotted, bile rising at the things this man did to those poor girls, and in some instances the crimes still unpunished.

With one hand, Cade held contact with Stan, yet held mine with the other. Just the feel of Cade's warmth gave me the strength to watch and dismiss the heinous acts. The incarcerated man was dying, and his twisted soul would suffer in the ultimate blackness.

An unnatural chill flooded my senses, and I clenched my jaw not to let my teeth chatter. This was it. It had to be, as it was the same unnatural chill that gripped my senses in Charlotte's spirit dive.

"Well, well. Who do we have here?" The whisper hit the back of my ear, its smooth menace clear. The creeper sensed me regardless of my passive role.

"Back off, asshole! Or I'll fry what's left of your pitiful life here and now." My words floated in the cold, but the weight of them put him in retreat.

"Mmmm… Such fire. Next time, sweetness."

"You won't have a next time, Stan Murphy. You sealed your fate in unsparing blackness the moment you gave your soul to the darkness."

His laugh made me want to throttle his skeletal form until his bones dislocated.

"Breathe, love. I got this one." Cade's Keeper guru powers hit full force, and the man's fetid mind filled with an iciness so cold it burned. Stan cried out, but the icy char was relentless, fueled by the cries and pleading of the women whose lives he destroyed.

One Scythe Fits All

The universe was pitiless in its karmic backlash. Swirling and gathering the pain and suffering of every one of his victims and lashing it back tenfold."

"Please...don't. No! STOP!"

"You turned a deaf ear to those girls, reveling in their pain and fear, and now the universe has turned the tables on you, you absolute horror of a human being."

The man retreated, but not before Cade caught the memory we sought. He held on with a finesse I had yet to master, all while keeping Stan at bay.

Stan stood at the bar, surveying the women on the dance floor. Most were with dates, but there were a few out with friends. A girls' night. He can't keep his eyes off one woman. Young. Maybe eighteen. Fresh. Ripe.

Draining his drink, he pushes back from the bar only to stop when another woman puts her hand on his arm.

"You don't want that one, Stanley." The woman's hand drifted from his arm to his chest. "She's too easy. To pliable. Her fear won't give you what you're looking for..." Her hand slid lower, stopping at just below his belt. "It will only whet what we both know is bubbling beneath the surface...here."

His face paled, but he licked his lips. Unable to tear his eyes away from the mysterious woman. "Who...who...are you? How do you know me?"

Polished and perfectly coiffed, her deep red lips promised as much as her sleek body, sheathed in a slinky black dress and kitten heels.

She stood from her barstool, letting her fingers toy with the tab to his fly. "I've been watching you, Stan. I think we can help each other."

"I don't need help!"

He tried for bravado but failed. "That's too bad," she tsked. "I had one little test to make sure you were the one. A test I think would be very...very...satisfying for us both." Her hand cupped his crotch, giving his growing erection a telling squeeze.

She released him, and without a backward glance, walked to the exit. Stan followed like a puppy.

"Where are you running to, sweetheart?" He grabbed her arm. "My car's parked in the back, and there's more than enough room for what you want."

"Oh really." She leaned against the building. "And you think you can give me what I want, huh?"

He was on her in seconds, and in less time than that, she had him on his back in the alley beside the bar. The same oily feel coated my senses as it did in Charlotte's spirit dive. This time, the shadowy mist swirled along the alley's edges, crawling serpentine-like until it enveloped them both as she rode Stan, her hands gripping each side of his head.

Stan's body shuddered beneath her straddle, his muscles undulating under his skin. She opened his mouth with her thumb, spitting something black and gelatinous into his throat.

He sputtered and choked, trying to free himself, but she forced him to swallow the dark muck. He stilled as though dead.

One Scythe Fits All

She leaned in and inhaled, sliding one hand over his chest like she did in the bar. Her eyes glowed an otherworldly blue, and when she raised her other hand, a scythe appeared in her grip. With another screech, she pierced his chest with the tip of her blade. The crack was pure darkness, and when she pulled her scythe from his chest, it glowed the same shimmering blue along its razor edge.

The scene shifted. Stan was back in the bar with his head on a table in a pool of drunken drool.

"Hey, buddy!" The bartender shook his shoulder. "We're closing up. Time to go."

Stan lifted his head from the table in a fog. "Where'd she go?"

"Where'd who go?"

"The woman I left with. Tall. Black dress. Sexy red lips."

The bartender shook his head. "Man, you been here all night sucking down rot gut. You ain't been with no woman, let alone a kitten like that."

The dark trace was palpable, and I didn't want to believe what I just witnessed. The black dress. The red lips…but more incriminating than anything were those glowing blue eyes. The same blue eyes I saw in the Historia et Archivi Mortuorem. That covert archive Angelica showed us before the coup attempt.

The big bad in the dark mist who compelled Stan and lord knows how many others to steal pieces of living souls was Morana. The Grim.

Chapter Seventeen

CADE AND I RELEASED STAN FROM our joint mind meld at the same time. The old man's back arched, and he sucked in a breath as though waking from suspended animation.

His eyes fluttered, and the parched tip of his tongue darted to papery lips. When his lids fully opened, his gaze locked on mine, and a slick, predatory grin curved on his mouth.

"Not a chance, dead man." Cade pushed me behind his hip. "Forget the drain, you piece of shit, you're circling the toilet and I'm here to make sure you're completely flushed."

Cade lifted his hand, holding it out as if gripping the man's throat. Murphy's eyes widened, and his hand flew to the neck of his hospital gown.

"This is karma, Stan. I'm simply channeling the energy you released into this world. The fear. The pain. The humiliation. The trauma and self-loathing your victims suffered after you broke them. It's suffocating, isn't it?"

The man gurgled a semblance of a response, and surprise, surprise, two tears escaped to his sunken cheeks.

"Remorse, Stan?" Cade tsked. "Far too little, and far too late. You don't even merit a second look. Your journey on this plane is over, and I'm glad you're conscious enough to feel the taste of what's waiting for you in the darkness. You will languish and writhe in the extreme, and the world will be a better place when you're dust."

The man pulled at the neck of his gown as if that would help. Cade wasn't inflicting pain. He just opened the valve. I must've missed the chapter in the level five handbook that taught revenge is best served cold. Or maybe this was Cade's special talent, like being a celestial lie detector.

I caught movement in the door from the corner of my eye and turned to see a young orderly outside the open hospital room door. He seemed perturbed, peering into the threshold. Thea's wards were still in full force, but maybe we'd overstayed our fifteen-minute welcome.

"Cade," I interrupted. "We've got company."

He took his eyes off Stan to glance across his shoulder to the door. "Huh. That didn't take long."

"What do you mean?"

"For the B-team to show up. That's got to be Stan's Keeper. The Memento Mori report said he had one already assigned."

Thea looked as well, getting up to dig in her bag for a fourth crystal. Bending, she placed it ahead of the others and then stood back, uneasy.

"What's wrong, T?" If she was worried, then we should be as well.

"Black obsidian is a truth stone. When placed ahead of certain wards, it reveals deception. I set this ward to allow for Keepers to enter the room's protected space, and THAT is no Keeper."

I moved to Thea's side, and there was no doubt. The nictitating lids. The sharp set to its teeth. That orderly was a higher level reaper in human guise. Was the darkness really that predictable or just that arrogant?

"Wow," I replied, watching the reaper watch me. "You predicted it, Cade. You said the darkness would try and reap Stan for their own purposes, and here they are as if on cue."

My hand instinctively went to the pendant resting against my skin beneath my shirt. The mosaic's surface was cool, but not icy, and definitely not splintering through me like it had in the past. Thea's ward had to be nearly impenetrable because I didn't feel a single tell. No heat. No energy sizzle. Not a trickle of sweat.

"You don't have to worry about going nuclear, Louisa." Thea put a hand on my arm. "I doubled up, and the wards are holding."

One Scythe Fits All

The reaper hissed at that, taunting me in the same double timbre as all higher level reapers. "This isn't over, Keeper. You and your witch can weave a tapestry of spells, and it won't matter. That man was marked years before either of you were born. He belongs to the darkness."

His attempted burn was nothing more than verbal posturing. "Points for the bipedal lizard," I replied with a slow, deliberate clap. "Stan Murphy *is* destined for the darkness, but not before he's stripped of all sentience. He'll be yours, but as useless as all canceled souls."

I moved to the very edge of Thea's wards, careful not to bump any crystals with my feet. "So much for an easy reap and scoring points with the big bad. Maybe tell The Grim to choose better next time."

The reaper paused with a double-lidded blink as if confused. It was then its mouth curved in yet another taunting smile. "I'll make sure to tell *her* just that when I report back." It turned on its heel, and in two steps, vanished.

Cade released Stan from the karmic backlash, and the man slumped against his pillow, gasping for breath. If possible, he seemed even more frail than when we first got here. His eyes fluttered once more and then closed. Stan was comatose again, and his machines beeped accordingly.

Thea bent to collect her crystals and release the invisibility spell, but then hesitated. "Do you want me to wait a bit in case the reptile comes back?"

Cade motioned for Thea to hold off. Stan's monitors were taking longer and longer to register signs of life, until the ECG toned a high, sustained beep. Stan had flatlined.

"Now, Thea!" He pointed at her to release the wards, and then looked at me. "Lock and load, Lou. In case our nictitating friend is stupider than he looks."

An alarm sounded, followed by the thud of running feet in the corridor. Nurses ran in ahead of the doctor, but they didn't do much except check for a pulse.

"Time of death, twelve forty-eight pm." The doctor read the clock above the staff whiteboard where Stan's DNR was clearly marked.

Cade had a small ghost box at the ready, and the moment Stan's ghost materialized beside the bed, he captured his corrupted soul and locked the box.

"We have a few things to finish first, but someone will be with you shortly to fill out the release forms for next of kin," a nurse informed, corralling us toward the hospital room door.

I put my hand up at that point. "We want nothing to do with that monster. Cremate him. Bury him in a pauper's grave. Whatever. He showed no mercy in life, so he deserves none in death."

We turned and left the ward in unison, leaving the poor nurse with her mouth open. She was just the messenger, and I was glad she wouldn't remember a thing once Thea released whatever hoodoo she used to gain us access to the prison.

One Scythe Fits All

Stan Murphy would get what he deserved in death and afterwards. There would be no life in his afterlife, and I couldn't wait to tell Charlotte.

We drove back to the city in relative silence, only stopping for fast food and a bathroom break. There was a lot to process, but one thing was crystal clear. It was time to tell Angelica. Memento Mori needed proof of our suspicions, and now we had it.

After three hours in the car, we waited for Angelica in her office. Her assistant, Margie, said she was out, but didn't offer anything further.

Being out could mean anything when it came to Angie, from grabbing a quick lunch, to being in another realm. Margie had always been fair about Angelica and her timeframes, and if we had to hunker down for the duration, I was pretty sure she'd tell us.

We'd only been waiting about twenty minutes, but it seemed like hours. I couldn't sit, so I paced. Cade scrolled on his cellphone, while Thea had her drawing pencils and sketch pad. I could busy myself with my phone as well, but doomscrolling social media wasn't the best choice in my current mindset.

I chewed my lip, walking back and forth in front of Angie's desk. Everything I saw in Stan's head pointed to Morana.

The Grim was always styled in chic couture, oozing sex appeal and sin at a price, yet I would never have glimpsed her true self if Cade and I hadn't been with Angie that day in the covert archive.

Nothing could be clearer. The Grim was hiding in plain sight while her machinations unfolded in deliberate phases.

I remembered that day in the archive like it was yesterday. A hooded dress with a plunging neckline, a cinched waist, and a full skirt that looked as though shredded with a switchblade. Her eyes glowed that same strange blue, and she held that same scythe, the one topped with a human skull with its curved blade protruding from its maw.

I stopped pacing and looked at Cade and Thea on the couch. "We need to get into that secret archive again. I'd bet dollars to donuts we'd find the truth why The Grim is revolting against the light."

"There's no way, Lou." Cade locked his phone, putting it on the coffee table in front of the couch. "Only celestials have access to that archive, and then only specific angels. Morana isn't even allowed without Angelica's prior knowledge and permission."

"Yet she was there *before* we got there with Angie. In fact, if memory serves, she was annoyed we kept her waiting."

I nervous-chewed the end of my thumb, turning to catch a glimpse of the setting sun in west facing windows across the street. The refracted light cast sunspots in a hazy arc across the building.

"Of course!" I stalked toward the windows behind Angie's desk. "It's so clear now."

"Lou, what are you talking about?"

One Scythe Fits All

I pivoted around, still agitated, but this time because I'd connected a couple of dots. "That blue shimmer along The Grim's scythe…and those blue bursts…they have to be from fractured pieces of souls."

"We can't know that for sure, Lou."

"Maybe not, but it kind of makes sense. Morana is using sparks of divinity to power her scythe!"

Cade looked at the sun on the building behind me, and I know he made the connection as well, but he still shook his head.

"Think about it Cade. When we untether souls from their earthly bonds, what color are they when we move them on?"

"They shimmer white."

"Exactly. White." I paced again. "Charlotte's soul was fractured, and a piece stolen. We both witnessed the incident in her spirit dive. What color did that piece glow in the reaper's grasp?"

"Blue."

"Right!" I stopped pacing and leaned on Angelica's desk, spreading my hands in a mic drop moment. "Legit souls glow white. Stolen ones glow blue. The same blue as The Grim's glowing eyes, and the same shimmer that emanates from her scythe."

"You'd think The Grim's eyes would glow red for hellfire and brimstone," Thea replied. "Blue is the world's favorite color. It's too optimistic for something so sly."

"It's also a color perceived as cold," I countered. "It's the color of depression, anxiety, and suicide."

"Thank you, Miss Debbie Downer."

"Lou may have a point, Thea. Green is considered a calming color, but it's also associated with jealousy. Two sides to the same coin, like Angelica and Morana. Though, I don't think we should ascribe much credence to the color of The Grim's eyes or her scythe. We're speculating again. Besides, the woman in Stan's memory who left the dark trace didn't look anything like Morana. Nor would Morana screw a paunchy human on the ground in a dirty alley."

Thea coughed, and we both turned to look at her. "If I didn't know you better, I'd swear you just coughed the word bullshit."

"Girl, if I have something to say, I'll say it. In truth, I'm not seeing the same connection as you. From what you're describing, it sounds like our boy Stan was attacked by a succubus in that alley."

"An energy vampire?" I asked.

"No. A succubus. A female demon who feeds off sexual energy and fluids. They prey on men, especially men with issues. Succubi are considered dream demons since they usually seduce men while they sleep in order to feed. Psychosis isn't uncommon in victims after an attack."

I chewed my lip again. "Except Stan wasn't asleep. He was about to target a young girl on the dance floor when our mystery lady interrupted his plans."

"I'm just saying, Louisa." Thea lifted a hand and then let it drop to her lap. "Maybe Morana is a secret shapeshifter and chose to embody a succubus."

One Scythe Fits All

"What are you three talking about? Morana is not a shapeshifter, nor a succubus." Angelica stood in the doorway to her office. "Someone needs to explain why I leave for a meeting with Michael only to come back to find three mouseketeers waiting in my office."

"Don't you mean musketeers?" Thea corrected and I cringed. Now was not the time.

"No, I meant it the way I said it, though I should have called you the three stooges. What is going on?"

I filled the Angel of Death in on what we discovered at the prison, including what Cade and I witnessed during Charlotte's spirit dive, and the similar wounds on ghosts in my yard.

"Angelica, as hard as it may be for you to accept, it all connects." I sat on the couch beside Cade, while Angie leaned on her desk looking very much like she debated sending the three of us permanently to limbo.

"Once again, my sister is many things, but she is neither a shapeshifter, a skin walker, nor a demon. Nor does she have glowing blue orbs for eyes. The trace you found in this attacker's mind, are you sure it's the same entity? Did you link it back to the black mist you originally saw?"

I nodded. "It carried the same oily feel. Moreover, this demon creature coughed up noxious phlegm and force fed it to the man. The M.O. is too similar to the way reapers attached themselves to Rose, putting her in the psych ward."

Angelica considered me, but she didn't comment. Whenever the Angel of Death went quiet, it never boded well.

"Couldn't we just contact Morana?" Thea suggested. "She's your sister. Wouldn't you be able to sense if she was up to something nefarious?"

Without responding, Angie walked around the end of her desk to sit in her leather chair. She quietly drummed her fingernails on the desk's glass surface, each tap-tap-tap ratcheting my anxiety.

"For crap's sake, Angie, YOU saw Morana's blue glowing orbs yourself!"

The drumming stopped, and Angelica's eyes found mine with a look that could freeze. I wasn't crazy and I wasn't backing down. I'd had enough of being gaslit. First bogus charges against me, then having my suspicions dismissed, but this took the cake.

"Angelica, we were together in that covert archive. Morana answered the door in her usual haute-du-slut couture, but the moment the archive door closed, she stood front and center in her Reaper garb. Black corseted bodice over a shredded gown, complete with hood and stiletto boots. She had glowing blue orb eyes, and her scythe glowed with the same blue shimmer. I did not imagine it."

I turned to look at Cade, and he nodded in agreement. "I saw it, too, Angie. Morana's true self."

My head bobbed like a doggie on a dashboard. "How do you not remember that? It was so in all our faces."

One Scythe Fits All

She folded her hands on the desk the way I'd seen dozens of times. I wouldn't say she believed us, but at least her incredulity was now suspicion. She opened a side drawer on her desk and took out what looked like a glass phone. Glass. As in a blinged out match to Cinderella's ball slippers.

She pressed a button on the screen, and white light circled the phone's edges until a man's voice answered.

"Michael, we have a problem…"

Chapter Eighteen

MICHAEL'S UNBLINKING attention unnerved me, as Cade and I rehashed everything we knew and what we suspected.

Leaving no detail overlooked, I leaned back on the couch, my shoulders slumping. Not because the archangel doubted us, but because I was exhausted from the enormity of what we discovered.

My heart broke for Angelica. The Grim was her sister, and though they were technically on opposing sides, they were still *sisters*. I still remember Angie's response when I learned about their familial connection.

I talk with Rani at least once a week. Unless she's pissing me off. What can I say? Sisters fight from time to time. Even the immortal ones...

One Scythe Fits All

I nearly fell off the couch then, and I felt the same sense of disbelief when I saw those glowing blue eyes in Stan's memory. Only this time my incredulity stemmed from betrayal. Not for me, but for Angie.

"Louisa, for the last time! I told you. The entity you saw wasn't my sister." Angelica was as nonplussed as the rest of us, and her reaction now was in direct response to Michael's lack thereof.

"Say something, dammit!" Her eyes blazed at Michael, and she slammed her palms on her desk. "You know Rani as well as I do, and you know her formal state. Hell, YOU'RE the one responsible for it."

I'd never heard Angelica raise her voice to this level. Not even when I pushed her on why she hadn't filled me in on what to expect at the inquest. This bordered on panicked with a shrill edge.

If the argument was between any other two, I'd sit back with a bowl of popcorn and watch the fireworks, but this was *our* Angelica. We needed to get to the bottom of this conundrum for her sake as well as Charlotte's, and my gut told me this went way deeper than simply soul-stacking for better odds.

"The Angel of Death has a point about The Grim's formal state," Michael replied, finally. "Though I beg to differ on responsibility."

Angelica inhaled, sliding her hand back to a composed fold on the desk. "Thank you, Michael. I'll say it again. Morana does not glow in any way, shape or form. Neither does her scythe. Her eyes are black in her Grim state and they're scary as hell."

She paused, looking at Cade and me. "There isn't anything I don't know about my sister. Her scythe was forged from ore mined from Abaddon's pit, so it's rather fetid. Like rotten eggs and body odor. It's staff was carved from the Tree of Wisdom, and the skull connecting the two belongs to the first to commit murder, or more specifically, fratricide.

Thea's mouth dropped. "You don't mean who I think you mean."

"If you thought Cain, then yes."

Even Cade seemed floored by the revelation. "As in the story of Cain and Abel?"

"What other Cain is there?" Angie dismissed our collective skepticism. "Look, the book with a capital B embellishes a lot, and humans have twisted its words for their own selfish purposes, but that gets sorted when they end up here facing their life's audit."

She exhaled. "Cain was the first of the human race cast into the darkness. It's why Rani has his skull on her scythe. It's all in the archive we visited."

"You mean the covert archive no one at Memento Mori can access but you?"

"Secret archive, Cade. Not covert. Covert makes it sound conspiratorial, but I see your point. I'll do what I can for you and Louisa."

"Angie, do I really need to be here for this ancient history lesson? We're off topic, and I have things to do. You called me to say we have a problem, and the question remains whether The Grim strayed from her mandated contract or not. I don't believe so, but let's revisit the facts.

"First, Morana di Mori, a.k.a The Grim, does not present in a glowing fashion, blue or otherwise. Glowing eyes are strictly a demonic trait…"

"And?" I interrupted. "Her title is *The Grim*. She works for the Darkness."

He turned silver eyes my way, and my bravado puckered along with my butt. "That doesn't mean anything, Louisa. Morana was created angel, not demon. Her being cast down was a mistake. A very costly, and very painful mistake."

He paused before continuing. "As I was about to say before being cut short, unlike her higher level reapers, shapeshifting is also not in The Grim's mandate."

The archangel was not happy with me, so I dialed it back. Especially since he still controlled my fate when it came to facing a tribunal or not.

"I understand all of the above, and I meant no disrespect. Morana and I have had our issues in the past, but I genuinely like her. Her mandate notwithstanding, it's unsettling to me to think she is behind this kind of suffering. She enjoys a challenge, and likes the taste of power, but she was always reasonable to an extent. At least with me."

Saying Morana was reasonable was a stretch, and everyone knew it. Including Michael. Did the white lie cast me in poor light? That remained to be seen, but I stretched the truth for Angie's sake.

"Add all of the above to what you and Angelica claim, and it still doesn't negate what Cade and I saw, or the fact a high level reaper showed at the prison hospital to snatch Stan's soul before he passed."

I shrugged. "Granted, it was only moments beforehand, but that begs two questions: one, how did that reaper know Stan was about to shuffle off this mortal coil, and two, where the hell was the Keeper assigned to the man?"

Michael went to reply, but I put up a hand, respectfully shutting him down. "My last question was for Angie as CEO of Memento Mori. Cade and I saw the record in the public archive. Stan Murphy was assigned a Keeper to ensure his soul was canceled before it was sent to the darkness. That Keeper never showed, so what would've happened if we hadn't been there at the allotted time?"

Cade nodded, eyeballing Michael. "Lou's point is valid, and it merits consideration. She's no longer a newbie, and in my long capacity as Keeper, I've seen my fair share of dark souls relegated to cancelation. I know the drill. Reapers do not show up before the event. They circle and they swoop once the soul has left the body. It's Keeper 101."

Cade had my back on this and other points. I was glad for the solidarity. Especially in this company.

"We all know reapers have flouted contract boundaries at times over the millennia," he continued. "But we don't believe Charlotte's case involving Stan, and this dark entity, is a one off. Not with thirty souls currently in Lou's charge with the same core withering as Charlotte. All proof points to The Grim, so unless you can provide another reasonable explanation, there's not much else to say."

Michael's chin dropped to his chest before he finally looked up. "Your proof is a purposeful red herring, or at least that's what I suspect. I'd have to examine the soul you secured for cancelation to be sure."

Cade pulled the spirit box he had at the prison hospital from his pocket and handed it to Michael.

"Good." He put the spirit box on Angie's desk, and then stood back. "Humans, shield your eyes. This will blind you otherwise."

Michael lifted his hands, and energy crackled in his palms same as it did in mine whenever angel fire threatened. "Shield your eyes, now!"

Of course, I peeked through my fingers, wincing at the piercing white light. When Michael gave the all clear, his studied gaze found mine. I braced for censure, but his expression was curious rather than annoyed.

The spirit box was encased inside a large, clear orb. With a flick of the archangel's hand, the box opened, and a dirty gray miasma spread from the interior, coating the orb with a nasty film.

"What is that?" I asked.

Michael's hand manipulated the miasma, until a sludgy form appeared. I expected Stan's ghost in miniature, instead it was a blob.

"Is that Stan?"

The archangel didn't take his eyes from the sludgy blob, but he shook his head. "It's his corrupted soul. Pure souls, or ones with relatively small amounts of smut, float. Blackened souls congeal, like this one. I don't like working with spectral forms. Especially in cases like this. I deal in facts, not emotion. The soul tells me everything I need to know. I leave audits and resolutions to Angelica and her Keepers."

"Don't you decide who moves on and who doesn't?" Thea's face was fascinated watching the sludgy blob.

"Nope," he replied. "You're confusing me with my brother, Uriel. He is the Archangel of Presence. My domain is maintaining the balance, which is why the dark trace you mentioned interests me."

His hand touched the clear orb and the sludge recoiled, but it quickly separated into hundreds of little globules.

Michael closed his eyes, and his whole body shimmered in gold and white light.

"He's entered a private realm," Angelica explained. "Each of those slimy balls is an event that led this soul to its corrupted state. Michael is sorting through them to find the origin trace."

The words were barely out of Angelica's mouth when Michael's eyes snapped open. A sound I never hope to hear again left the archangel, and the orb went nuclear, incinerating everything inside to nothing. Not even ash.

We were all on our feet after that, stunned. "Michael!" Emotions got the better of me and I shouted at the archangel. "THAT was evidence! Stan needs to pay for his crimes against all those women!"

Michael's face was a slash of anger, and Cade put his hand on my arm, ready to push me behind his hip the way he did in the prison hospital.

One Scythe Fits All

"Do you think I could witness that level of serial assault and death, and not make him pay? Rest assured he is paying and will continue to pay every second of eternity."

"Well?" Angelica wrung her hands, something she never did. "Was it Rani? Is she behind this betrayal?"

I held my breath for her.

"It was not Morana."

At those four words, Angelica and I exhaled at the same time. A weird mix of confusion and relief flooded my gut, but Angie's face was a mask of anger.

"Then who is impersonating my sister?"

It was Michael's turn to puff out an exasperated breath. "Lilith."

Thea pumped one fist in the air. "I knew it! I said it sounded like a succubus attacked Stan, and Lilith is that and more."

I looked from Thea to Cade before turning to Michael again. "You're sure it's Lilith. The same demon we read about as hooking up with Sam…"

Angie jerked her hand to my mouth, and I bit off the last of my sentence. "Not another word. I don't want his name on your lips. You are already too involved, but to answer your question, yes, he is involved with that she-devil."

"So why would Lilith want to impersonate Morana to orchestrate stealing pieces of souls?" Cade was as nonplussed as the rest of us.

Michael's eyes found the pendant hanging at my neck, and I shook my head. I was not taking the rap for this. "Forget it, Michael. You're wrong." I lifted the pendant, and it warmed in my hand as if telling me to go for it. "This was created by Keepers, *for* Keepers, and nothing more."

"Exactly," he replied softly. "It was created as a conduit to my light."

I made a sound like a gameshow buzzer. "Wrong again. Emmie wore this pendant before me, and there's a line of Keepers before her who wore it as well. No one has channeled angel fire except me. So, it's not the pendant."

Had I just incriminated myself, handing Michael a reason to relegate me to a tribunal? At this point, I didn't care. Cade and I would find a way, even if it meant threatening the entire celestial system with what we knew.

"You are one hundred percent correct, Louisa. It is not the pendant in and of itself. Angel fire happens when the pendant is paired with the correct bearer." He pointed at me. "You."

"Me?"

He nodded. "I could test your blood, but I don't need to. Your own curiosity and disregard for rules gave me all the proof I need."

"Test my blood," I repeated, thrown.

Angelica put a hand on my arm. "Angel blood shimmers gold, and those with trace angel blood in their veins will present with gold flecks under the right conditions."

One Scythe Fits All

I knew where Michael was headed, and I refused to consider the possibility. It was nuts.

"Nope. You're wrong."

"Louisa, you watched my light nearly engulf this entire space. You defied the safety measures I asked of the three humans in this room, yet you stand before me unharmed. Your vision is intact, as is your mind. Two very telling facts."

His smile made me shiver. Not from being creeped out, but because I knew in my gut he spoke truth.

"You are a scion, Louisa." Angelica's words were very soft. "I had my own suspicions when you were able to conduct spirit dives with such precision and ease, but it was when you wielded angel fire and merged with the universal divine that I knew. I just didn't know how to tell you. So much has been thrown at you in such a short time. Why else do you think I was so upset about your inquest? You're right. The charges against you are bogus, and *my* gut finally agrees with yours. This is all connected."

Michael nodded in agreement. "You three will have to forgive us for not seeing any of this. Angels can sense so many things, that we are often overwhelmed and become desensitized to the obvious."

"Desensitized. Isn't it concerning that a demon gained access to your sanctum archive right under Angelica's nose? Plus, we need to circle back to this scion thing once this is done and dusted."

"It is concerning, yes," Michael accepted. "As to you being a scion, it's simple. At some point in your bloodline, one of your ancestors was angelic. There's no way to trace who, or how, or why. What's important is it explains your ability to wield angel fire. Yes, your ability seems linked to my light stash and my particular gifts, but I don't think that matters.

"What matters is the darkness and what it wants with that pendant." He paused with his fingers laced, and his two index fingers resting on his lips. "My gut is now in concurrence with yours and Angelica's. I don't have all the answers, but my guess is the sporadic soul stealing attempts of the past were because the pendant was only a rumor. Now they know it's a reality. They've seen its power and are trying to replicate it."

"Bully for them." I snorted my contempt. "Maybe the darkness should consider giving up part of themselves and forge their own power source…oh wait, they can't because they have no souls."

"You are going to have to give up that pendant in order to reestablish the balance, Louisa."

I clicked my cheek at the archangel. "I don't think so. Not until we stop Lilith, prove that she's behind this debacle, and find those missing souls. Too many spirits are bound to this plane indefinitely because of her. They are rotting from the inside out, even after death. It's not fair, and if this pendant gives me one up on Lilith, then so be it."

I shook my head slowly, thinking.

"You've got that wheel turning look on your face again," Cade said. "Do you sense something?"

"No exactly, but I'm not buying Lilith doing this for no reason." I shook my head even more. "This scheme is sophisticated. Based on the decade range of the spirits with core withering in my charge, she's playing the long game. But why? What's her reasoning for doing so?"

Angelica and Michael shared a look that I wasn't about to let go. "Tell me."

Cade got up to stand with me, and then Thea joined him. With the three of us standing in solidarity, they couldn't ignore us.

"What you accidentally discovered during your spirit dive with Charlotte is a plot so deep it delves to the heart of Hell."

"Abaddon?" Cade asked.

Angelica and Michael's faces were like stone. "No," she answered first. "Samael."

Nervous laughter twittered from Thea, and I gripped her hand. We'd heard that name in the archive. Ruler of Hell. Apprehension radiated from her, and I didn't blame her for being tense.

"Have I inadvertently opened a can of hell hound treats?" I asked, trying to joke away the pit in my stomach. "Are they coming for me, teeth bared and drooling?"

A soft, close-lipped smile graced Michael's serious face. "Play them some music and they'll fall asleep."

Angelica must've told him my fondness for the Harry Potter series, and I appreciated the attempt at lightness.

"If my guess is correct," he said, getting back to the point, "the reason for Lilith's behavior is both petulant as well as dangerous. Not that she would care. Demons are selfish by nature."

I winced when Thea tightened her grip. "Great. So, what do you suggest we do?"

"You asked why Lilith is playing the long game. Two reasons. Jealousy and the desire for power. It's common knowledge Morana and I had a thing before she was cast down. Samael, being who he is, set his sights on her once Morana was under his authority."

"And?"

He spread his hands. "Lilith is Samael's established lover, but she is not his queen. Morana was created angel, and like I said, being cast down doesn't change that fact. A boon for the ruler of Hell. Being the jealous type, Lilith isn't one to put up with a rival who could possibly unseat her."

I couldn't believe my ears, and obviously neither could Thea. "Are you kidding me?" she blurted, letting go of my hand. "I've heard of high school hell, but this is ridiculous!"

"What do you think happens when a jealous demon who wants to be Queen of Hell finds she has a rival and too much time on her hands?" Michael's face was deadpan. "Samael is my archenemy. He has no skin in this celestial standoff because he didn't give Lilith an order to act. I don't have proof, but I know Samael like I know myself.

One Scythe Fits All

"Lilith has been at his side forever, and she knows how much he covets that pendant around your neck, Louisa. Up until now, it's been impossible to track or to even prove its existence. He's been experimenting, and Lilith is all too happy to oblige his hobby. Even if he didn't explicitly say.

"My guess is Samael is sitting back with his popcorn, watching Lilith's machinations with gusto. If she's successful, then Morana is removed, and Lilith is happy. Happy lover happy life. And he's pleased because he gains a weapon. All with the added bonus of being a thorn in my side and making the light the scapegoat."

This was a lot to take in, but at least all the dots connected. "Angie," I began. "When was the last time you spoke with Morana? Saw her?"

Angelica's expression pained as if finally fathoming the time. "Months. Not since the conservatorship was put in place."

Her eyes flashed as soon as the implications set in, and her hands clenched at her sides. "We've got a traitor in our midst, Michael. Rani would never NOT get word to me, and I'm to blame for my own inattention."

"Who is her conservator?" Cade was in sync with my same thoughts.

Angelica looked at Michael before answering. "Zach."

Chapter Nineteen

"ZACH?" THEA QUESTIONED. "Isn't that a rather modern name for an archangel conservator?"

Angelica shrugged, digging through files Margie had brought in on the guardianship. "It's short for Zachariel. He's a lower archangel and he's supposed to be a warden of judgment, but he's always been a little too much of a sycophant for my taste." Her eyes lifted to Michael. "Especially where certain angelic powerhouses are concerned."

"This is not my fault, Angie. Stop it."

She drew in a deep breath, and I knew she was counting to ten in her head. If anyone had the legal lowdown on this Zach, it was Angelica, and there was no way he'd escape her consequences if he was the one who brokered her sister for his own ends.

One Scythe Fits All

"You're right, Michael. What's important now is we locate Morana. My stomach is twisting with how abandoned she must feel."

"I think I might be able to help with that." Thea opened her large duffle, rummaging inside.

Between crystals and reptile skins, plus her regular paraphernalia, that bag had to weigh thirty pounds if it weighed an ounce. "Are you channeling your inner Mary Poppins, T? I half expect you to pull out a bloodhound to sniff one of Morana's couture outfits."

"Why would we need a bloodhound when you've got me?" She pulled a small pouch from the bag, and from the pouch a yellow mineral that looked an awful lot like gold. "I'm going to find The Grim."

Angelica put down the papers in her hand. "Rani is most likely in another realm, Thea. There's no way your human gifts, no matter how splendid, could pinpoint her there."

"I don't doubt that, Angie," Thea replied. "What I doubt is everyone assuming Morana will be hard to locate." She put the pendulum back in the pouch, and then put the pouch in her pocket.

"Thea, you can't scry for anyone with your dowsing crystal in your pocket." I lifted my hand, gesturing toward her boho skirt as if obvious. "Besides, don't you need a map to start?"

"I'm not going to scry for Morana. Not in the usual way, anyway. For this I need chalcopyrite, a yellow, sulfide mineral better known as fool's gold. The sulfur in the pyrite to help protect us, and a little help from some friends in the know to point us in the right direction." She dug in her bag again, only this time she pulled out two bags of sour gummy worms.

I laughed, finally getting her meaning. "Brilliant!"

Cade's face was confused at first, and then it dawned on him as well. "Good God, Thea. We should've thought of this two hours ago!"

"Will one of you insane people tell us what you're talking about?" Angelica crossed her arms, looking to Michael for help.

"Don't look at me."

Cade fished in his pocket for a handful of single dollar bills. "The gargoyle's, Angie. They hear everything, see everything, and know everything that happens at Memento Mori and in the other realms. We've just wasted precious time talking in circles, when we could be on the roof getting answers."

"The roof? Gargoyles don't speak, and they're vicious little beasties. They'd sooner eat your face than let you into their domain."

Thea sniffed at that. "I've been having lunch with the gargoyles since I got back from Italy after these two got engaged. They're protective of each other, and yes, they can be aggressive, but they are sweet as pie once you show them respect and earn their trust." She eyed the Angel of Death. "Haven't you ever tried to befriend them? Or are they just useful beasts to you, with a job to do and no more?"

One Scythe Fits All

Angelica was slack-jawed and speechless, something I never thought I'd see. She didn't seem angry. Just stunned.

Michael gave a chin pop toward the gummy worms. "Why the sweets?"

"They're Bix and Eddu's favorites. If we want their help, it's best to come bearing gifts."

Cade gestured with the singles in his hand. "I'll head down to the newsstand on the corner and get more gummy candy and then meet you on the roof.

"Let's think about this for a minute," I said, stopping everyone cold. "I am not climbing that death trap spiral staircase again, so someone better tell me there's another way.

Thea looked at me confused. "I have no idea what spiral staircase you're talking about. I just take the elevator."

My head jerked around to look at Angelica, and the woman had the nerve to flash me a sheepish grin. "What can I say? Sacrifice is good for the soul."

Now it was my turn to be slack-jawed and speechless.

"I'm kidding," she said, stuffing papers back into Margie's files. "Do you really think I'd climb a staircase like that in my heels if I didn't have to? There's the roof, and then there's *The Roof*. It's a separate dimension from the rest of Memento Mori, and the only way to facilitate a realm jump."

Thea angled her head at me, and I knew from the look on her face she had a hundred questions spawned from those two words. Realm jump.

I'd tell her later, but right now we needed enough gummy treats to keep the information flowing from Thea's bristly, yet soft, cat-like friends.

"I'm going to take your word for it Angelica," I replied. "One, because I have no choice, and two, because it doesn't matter at the moment."

The angel opened her purse and handed Cade a folded wad of cash. "Go down to the cafeteria and ask for Cedric. Tell him I sent you, and I'd like a case of chewy candy." She gestured toward the money. "That should cover it."

"Sour gummy worms and Swedish fish," Thea advised as Cade took the money and headed for the door. "Anything else might be hit or miss."

We waited for Cade to get back, and the five of us took the elevator to the roof. It opened to a concrete anteroom with a short, straightforward staircase leading to a reinforced door with the words ROOF stenciled in block letters on the metal.

Thea went first, then me and Cade, with Angelica and Michael bringing up the rear. We stopped behind Thea with her hand on the door handle.

"Let me go first. It's dark out, and this is not the usual time I visit. They're very sweet, but very much creatures of habit, and showing up unexpectedly might throw them. I don't want them upset, nor do I want to jeopardize my friendship with them."

One Scythe Fits All

No one had a problem with that.

"Good." She nodded. "They may only agree to speak with Louisa, maybe Cade. They know she's my friend and that she's engaged to marry Cade." Thea looked at Angelica and Michael. "You two, I can't say. You're archangels, and that's intimidating to them. They know you don't approve of fraternization."

Angie took offense to that. "Don't approve? I didn't even know they spoke or interacted in any way other than minor movement."

"Did you ever bother to ask or find out more?" Thea wasn't trying to be rude, and the question was valid.

Angie's face was a little red, but she kept her cool and simply nodded. "Whatever they want is fine, but please tell them the sweets were from me as a token of my appreciation."

"That I can do, and I will make sure they know that the gift is sincere." Thea took one of the boxes of candy from Cade, and then gave me a quick nod before opening the door. "Bix! Look what I brought you guys…"

We waited behind that metal door for what seemed like hours. Cade opened one of the other boxes of sweets, and I took two bags of Swedish fish and polished them off without thinking twice. The only thing better would've been a fruit and nut chocolate bar, and before I finished my thought, Cade handed me my favorite.

"I know you, Lou. In case of emergency, bring chocolate." He tilted my chin up and I gave him a sugary kiss.

"Louisa!" Thea called from the other side of the door. The door opened about ten inches, and she grabbed my arm. "Squeeze through. I don't want them seeing who else is here until they're ready."

"What about Cade?"

She shook her head. "Just you."

I spared him a quick look and he nodded. "Go. You'll be fine. Explain what we need. We'll be waiting in the office. If they want to meet anyone else, just text me."

"Okay." I kissed him again, and then wiggled through the door.

It shut behind us with a thud. "Are you sure it doesn't lock from this side?"

"I opened it to get you, didn't I?" Thea whispered, and then glanced over her shoulder. "I hope Cade left the rest of the candy."

As if reading my mind, my phone dinged with a text notification and a heart emoji: Candy is on the roof steps. 💚 You got this.

I followed Thea toward the edge of the roof facing Madison Avenue. To think I'd jumped off this same roof in a different dimension into another realm just a few days earlier was mind boggling. Almost as mind boggling as walking with my best friend to talk to actual gargoyles.

One Scythe Fits All

We stopped about ten feet from the concrete parapet where five life size statues perched facing the street. Before I could say a word, two of the five turned, awakening before our eyes.

"Bix… Eddu… I know it's late, and I don't mean to pull you from your duties, but I've brought my friend Louisa Jericho to meet you."

Thea put the box of gummy candy down on the rooftop and then opened the cardboard lid for them to see the contents. "This is a token from Angelica in both apology and gratitude for our unexpected visit. There are more boxes waiting for you inside." She gestured toward the reinforced metal door.

Bix and Eddu inclined their heads. Was that approval or just acknowledgment?

Both gargoyles were putty gray in color, and they looked as wrinkly soft as Thea described. The difference was in their face structure. Bix's face was long, with a heart-point chin, while Eddu's face was square with a wide mouth.

They both had large, cat-like ears that twitched in different directions, and teeth that would make the devil himself think twice. Pigeons venturing near the roof didn't stand a chance. One bite and boom! Split breast birds. Like air jaws.

At least the stockpile of bones Thea warned about had been picked clean, and in some cases sun-bleached, or I wouldn't have been able to ignore them.

It was unnerving how inanimate they seemed sitting on the parapet. Feet curled, gripping the concrete lip, their wings folded on their back, and their terrifying mouths partly open as if scenting the wind.

I took in their monstrous faces, and the saying, they're so ugly they're cute, ran through my head. Not that I'd say anything so stupid.

"Louissssssa."

The protracted hiss in Bix's greeting wasn't unpleasant. He followed it with a slow blink, and I wondered if that was another form of acknowledgment or if we had woke him.

"It's a pleasure to make your acquaintance, Bix." I hoped I put the right name with the right gargoyle. "Am I supposed to slow blink back?" I whispered, but Thea quietly shook her head.

Before I could ask anything else, Bix opened his wings and jumped to the rooftop. When I say jumped, it was more of a stealth yet graceful glide, landing without a sound on the mastic rooftop. Again, those poor pigeons.

These gargoyles were about four feet in height, but Bix's bat-like wings spread in a span three times that. Eddu's were equal in size. I saw that when he spread his wings to swat at bugs attracted to the security lights.

Bix sat with his front paws together. His hindquarters were heavily muscled, and despite his feline bearing, he reminded me of a flying monkey from the *Wizard of Oz*.

"Gummiesssssss?"

Thea nodded. "Sour worms, red fish, and something new. Gummy sharks."

One Scythe Fits All

Curious, the gargoyle opened the bag of blue and white sharks. His hands were clawed and paw-like, but on closer look they were more like otter's hands. Nimble and dexterous, with opposable thumbs.

Bix put one large gummy shark in his mouth and chewed, making a sound that was a cross between a gulp and a yummy noise.

"I think he just found a new favorite," I whispered.

"I hope not. Those things aren't cheap."

"They're a gift from Angie, remember? She can keep Bix and his buddies in every species of underwater maneater if need be."

Bix swallowed, and when he smiled there were bits of blue candy stuck in his teeth. "Good ssssshshshark, but not sssssssour."

I nodded, making a mental note to tell Angie. With no idea how to broach the topic of Morana, I gave Thea the high sign. We were burning moonlight and we needed to get going.

"Bix, we need your help," she prefaced, squatting to dig in the box for the largest bag of sour worms we had.

The gargoyle angled his large head, watching. He whistled low, and the sound was like a zephyr breeze, soft and encouraging.

"You want to find the sisssssster," he responded, swallowing another shark.

I took that as a good sign. "Yes. It's important. If I don't find her, I may be to blame for her disappearance."

It was far more complicated than that, and I was hoping Thea was right when she said gargoyles heard and saw everything.

Bix chewed, ending up with more sticky candy in his teeth. When he reached for a bone to pick them clean, I had to look at my feet.

"Gargoylessssss know what happened to Louissssssa. Bixxxxxx knowssssss. The demon hasssss the sisssssster."

My head popped up at that, bone-picking sticky bits be damned. "You mean Lilith." It wasn't a question.

The gargoyle's face creased at the name, but he bobbed his head.

"Do you know where the demon has the sister?" Thea asked, gently handing him a bag of the sour worms.

Bix didn't refer to Morana by name, and Thea followed suit. Was it against gargoyle rules to speak angelic names or was it just sass? If it was sass, it only made me like Bix all the more. Teeth-picking aside.

"Yesssssss, Bixxxxxx knowssssss. The demon has the sisssssster in the underworld."

I blinked watching the gargoyle shove the entire bag of gummy worms into his mouth, cellophane and all.

"The underworld," I repeated, giving him a chance to chew. "Do you mean the place we call the darkness?"

Underworld sounded mythological, as in the story of Hades and Persephone. I needed to know what he meant for certain.

One Scythe Fits All

"The darknesssssss." He nodded. "Ssssssome call the placccccce Hell."

"Do you know where in the darkness the sister is being held?"

Bix stopped chewing, and then turned his large, round eyes to me. If Michael's unblinking stare was unnerving, this one had me choking on my tongue.

"It's okay, Louisa. That stare is just a gargoyle's way of feeling you out. You're not in any danger. Trust me. If his hackles were up we'd be running for cover, but he's just taking you in."

"Like deciding how I'd compare to the taste of pigeon?"

She rolled her eyes at that. "No, dummy. He's evaluating you. Your body language. Your scent. He's gauging how much to tell you and if you can be trusted."

I swear I saw Bix's flat nostrils flare, and I wondered what my spike in adrenaline smelled like to him. Salty? Or maybe I smelled like candy. I gulped at the prospect.

"You said they like to gossip. Maybe I should spill a few Memento Mori morsels and take his mind off why we showed up unannounced."

Thea chuckled. "You could try, but it's usually *them* who spill the tea."

I had an idea. I wasn't sure Cade would like it, but the gargoyle needed to throw us a bone, and I didn't mean pigeon.

"Bix," I interrupted his scent-o-meter eval. "Would you like to come to my wedding? We're thinking of having it on the roof of my brownstone, so there's plenty of places to perch. Angelica has offered to officiate, so there should be lots of interesting tidbits, even if it is a small affair."

That got the gargoyle to blink. He even stopped chewing and swallowed the gummy wad in his mouth whole.

"Louisssssa meanssssss thissssss?"

I nodded. "Absolutely. Who wouldn't want to be the first to have a hunky gargoyle at their wedding? You can even bring a plus one if you like. Reality TV would scream for something that juicy."

The gargoyle smiled, and this time the grin went from pointy ear to pointy ear. "Bixxxxxx will be guessssssst? No guard?"

"You will be *my* guest. I haven't sent out the invitations yet, but I will deliver yours personally."

Bix glanced over his wing at his brother and then looked back. "Eddu ssssssstuck here. He can't be guesssssst."

I didn't know what he meant, but I wasn't going to ask. "But you can come, yes?"

He nodded. "Bixxxxxx can." He walked closer and I planted my feet where I stood. If I recoiled now, it was game over.

The gargoyle's footsteps were padded and silent, but the weight and width of his wings gave his gait a bit of a waddle. He reached a hand toward mine, and I didn't flinch or hesitate taking the proffered gesture.

"Louissssssa Jericho is friend." He kissed my hand, and the feel was tickly and a little wet.

One Scythe Fits All

"Thank you, Bix."

With my hand still in his paw, he looked up at me. "The sissssssster is in the Keeper's room." His gaze fell to my pendant. "A traitorsssss room in the darknesssss."

Why did he look at my pendant and then refer to a traitor?

Bix looked up again. "Look for the rulerssssss lair firsssssst. The otherssssss will guide you."

His gaze fell to my pendant again, but before I could ask him to clarify, he released my hand and then lofted to the parapet. His back was to us once more, and he resumed his stony posture, leaving Thea and I both with unanswered questions.

"C'mon," she said, gathering up what was left of the candy and the wrappers Bix didn't eat. "We'll save the rest for another day."

"But..."

She tugged my arm. "He's done talking, Louisa. You've been marked as a friend, so leave it there. He told us all he was willing to tell, so push for more and you won't be a friend for long. You might even find yourself dropped from very sharp claws onto Madison Avenue."

I shut up and followed her back to the roof door. We piled the remaining boxes of candy to one side of the concrete stairs, and then got in the elevator.

"We need to tell everyone what the gargoyle said, and hopefully we can figure out the traitor's identity."

"Yeah," Thea agreed, "but first we need to figure out how to get into the underworld or darkness or whatever you call it."

The elevator dinged and we walked out onto Angie's office floor. "That's the easiest part, T."

"Are you telling me you know how to find the entrance to Hell?"

I smiled. "I do. It's in Penn Station."

Chapter Twenty

"WHY DID BIX LOOK AT MY PENDANT when he said the word traitor? Then again when he said the others would guide me the rest of the way?" I made a face. "Gargoyles are definitely part of the celestial set, or at the very least, they're related, because they love to talk in cryptic."

Angelica held out her hand, and I knew what she wanted. I took the pendant from my neck and halfheartedly put it in her palm. I had promised Cade. If Angie asked for the pendant, I would give it to her.

I kept my word, but that didn't help the sudden rush of naked vulnerability. Maybe all the joking about it being my superpower wasn't unfounded.

Angie held the pendant like a sandwich between her palms. With her eyes closed, she muttered ancient words. A white and gold shimmer engulfed her hand, same as Michael before he decimated Stan's sludge.

Panic gripped my gut and I had to sit on my hands to stop from snatching the pendant back. Ugh, I really was Gollum.

"Angie, please..."

One look from Michael shut me down, as if reminding me if Angelica wanted to destroy the pendant, then who was I to say no?

Her eyes opened, and so did her hands. Except for a residual glow, the pendant was intact. I wish I could say the same about Angelica's expression. It was a mix of grief, hurt, and anger.

"Angelica?" Michael asked, moving to put his hand on her shoulder. "What did you see?"

She craned her neck to meet his concerned gaze. "I know who our traitors are."

"Traitors," I repeated. "As in more than one?"

She nodded, handing me back the pendant. "Put that on and don't take it off until I tell you to do so. The gargoyle was correct. It's our only link to finding my sister."

Sitting back in her chair, she pressed the intercom.

"Yes, Angie?"

"Margie, send Zach in asap. I don't care where he is, he's to get here immediately."

"He's in the building, ma'am. In the archive."

Angelica hesitated a moment. "The public archive?"

"Yes. I'll send a message down right now."

I went to question her, but Angie waved me quiet. "Thea, what crystals do you have in your duffle? I want a protective circle that will keep the person captive until I release them."

"Angie, white magic doesn't work that way. I can keep harm out, but I've never cast a circle to keep harm in."

"Thea, I'm not explaining myself well. In a few minutes, Zach is going to walk through my office door. Margie will give me a heads up when he arrives, but I need to keep him in a place where he can do no harm. He's one of our traitors."

The witch nodded, opening her bag. "I get it. You want to bind him. That I can do."

"Isn't your office already protected?" Cade asked. "I was under the impression it was under a celestial ward that exposed deceit as well as demonic bonds."

She nodded. "It is, but if what I suspect is true, there's a loophole being exploited."

"What's your plan, and how can we help?" Cade stood, moving to help Thea sort through her witchy items.

"Nothing right now, but thanks." She turned, and Michael met her gaze. "You know what I mean to do, and what I need to do it, right?"

"I don't like this, Angelica. It puts me in a very difficult position."

She rolled one shoulder and it cracked audibly. "I can't do this without your permission, Michael. You know that."

My eyes ping-ponged between the two archangels.

"Angie, it puts me on the same level as Samael. I won't do that."

The flat of her hands hit the desk and she stood from her chair. "Then leave and I'll do this without your consent. You know it's the only way, and for you to use that cop out is unconscionable after everything that's been done to my people over five hundred years." She ticked off events on one hand. "Penny. Cade. Rose. The fractured souls that span the past century, and they're just the tip of the iceberg. Then the damage to Morana…" Her hand flew out toward me. "and Louisa!"

"Angelica."

She wasn't having it. "Look your scion in the face and tell *your* descendant you won't help."

Wait. What?

Every activity stopped and all eyes turned to the two angels in the room.

"I'm sorry, what?" I asked, getting to my feet as well. "Michael said there was no way to trace the how, why, or when of my scionhood."

"He wasn't wrong about that, but he's skirting the most telling trait. You channel HIS fire. His light. No one else would be able to do so if you didn't share his bloodline, even in trace amounts. Millenia ago, angels were more open to experiences. It was only after Lucifer pulled his 'better to reign in Hell than serve in Heaven' bullshit that the universal hammer came down."

I sat again, stunned for the second time into silence.

One Scythe Fits All

"Give it up for Louisa's one thousand times great grandpappy."

I shot Thea a look, but then burst out laughing. This was too ludicrous a scenario not to at least chuckle.

"I'm so glad you find your angelic trace worthy of such levity." Michael sniffed.

"Get over yourself, Grandpa. If I am your scion, then you need to step up and help us. You need to do whatever Angie needs. Forget my bloodline. Do it because you know it's the right thing to do. Kind of part of the angelic mandate, remember?"

I knew all about the *angels are legion* schtick, but as blinded, bogged down, and desensitized as they had become, they still weren't the darkness.

"Fine. You have my consent." Michael inhaled, giving Angie a quick nod. "BUT I need to be here so there's no question."

I snort grimaced. "Who's kicking you out, big guy?"

One look told me I was skating on thin ice with the archangel, but I was beyond it. If he planned to tell me partial truths, then he could deal with the fallout.

Ignoring me, he circled his hand and two spirit boxes unlike any I'd seen before materialized in his palm. They were gold, and trimmed in a pearlescent white, but that's not what made them so unique. It was their size. They were tiny. Like they belonged on a shelf inside a dollhouse.

"Perfect, Michael." Angie took them from him. "Thank you."

"If you needed spirit boxes, I always carry a couple in my backpack, Angie. You just had to ask," Cade offered, moving the coffee table out of the way to set up Thea's circle.

Michael sat in his chair in front of Angie's desk, swiveling to watch. "The kind of spirit box needed for what Angie wants to do has to be one from my realm, Cade."

"Why?" I asked. "What are you planning?"

Angie's face was deadpan. "To separate Zach's divinity from his human form. It's not easy, but it's the only way I can get to the bottom of how he managed to double cross me, my sister, Michael, and use a Keeper who sacrificed part of her soul in the pendant around your neck."

All activity stopped again, and we looked at Angelica.

"I don't want to get into how I did so or how I know, but I was able to read the Keepers' souls who sacrificed bits of their own spark to create that pendant. I was able to read not only the pieces of their souls in the mosaic, but their waiting state in limbo. It didn't take much to pinpoint the weakest link."

I held my breath while she spoke, but now I needed to know. "Please tell me it wasn't Emmie."

"No, my friend. It's not our beloved Emily. It's a Keeper named Arabella. She died around the time of the American Revolution and has been pining in limbo."

"Let me guess. Zach."

She nodded at me. "He's a lower level archangel, so he has access to limbo and other celestial realms. With him being appointed my sister's conservatorship, he gained access to the darkness as well."

"So, an all access pass," Cade replied.

"For lack of a better way of describing it, yes."

I looked at Michael swiveling casually in his chair. "And there were no red flags. No disturbances in the force. Nothing to give you a heads up something was amiss. Not in five hundred years since the first souls were snatched before their time during the plague. Not when Penny reported it here. Not when soul after soul after soul were documented with core withering. Nothing."

Michael's eyes held mine, but I wasn't about to blink first. He inhaled, and then glanced away.

"I'm going to take that as a yes, 'I'm sure there were red flags, Louisa, but we were too nose blind to sniff them out.'"

Michael's gaze jerked back to me for a moment before switching to Angelica. "Is she always like this?"

"Pretty much, yes."

Cade moved to lean over my chair and press a kiss to my temple. "It's one of her best traits."

"Done." Thea stood back from her circle work. "Black tourmaline and obsidian, augmented by selenite should do the trick. I've drawn a vague outline of a circle with a pentacle with salt chalk on the rug, but that can be vacuumed later."

"A pentacle." Michael squatted at the edge of the circle. "I never thought I'd see the day."

Thea shrugged. "It's about intention, Michael. Our intentions are based in the light, not the dark. Easy peasy, celestial squeezy. It's all good."

"Her, too?" He looked over at Angie again.

Angie grinned this time. "Yes, Michael. Her, too."

The buzzer on the intercom sounded and Margie's voice told us Zach was here. Angelica waved a hand over the crystals, and they blended into the carpet. They were still there and still potent, just camouflaged.

"Send him in."

Zach opened the door, hesitating in the threshold. "Wow, Margie didn't tell me this was party. I wouldn't have come empty handed."

He chuckled at his own joke, but his face was apprehensive. Guess traitor boy wasn't as stupid as he looked.

"Zach. Thank you for coming so quickly. The room is a little crowded, so I'd appreciate if you remain standing." Angelica pointed to the rug where the coffee table used to be."

The moment he stepped over the circle threshold, the crystals lit, trapping him inside. Angie opened the first of the celestial spirit boxes, and she and Michael chanted the ancient whispers together.

Heaven spawned.
Heaven loved.
Divine creation sowed above.

One Scythe Fits All

The light within.
Divinity enshrined.
Corrupted by the force of time.
Follow none and will be done.
Separate parts no longer one.

I don't know how I understood the chant. Maybe it was the angel blood ignited in my veins, but the ancient intonation resonated.

Zach gripped his middle, falling to his knees. "Why are you doing this?" he ground out.

When he looked up he saw Michael and then the golden spirit box in Angelica's palm.

"Don't do this! I was under compulsion! It's Lilith's fault! She did this to me!"

A shimmering gold and white light peeled from his body like a second skin. Each inch of separation, agony. I had to turn away. The man had betrayed the light and had done his part to sentence so many souls to a withering death, but it was still hard to watch.

The ethereal light trailed in a glistening line to the golden spirit box which snapped closed when the deed was complete. Zach curled in a ball at the center of Thea's circle, whimpering.

"Zachariel." Michael's voice boomed, and I had to put my fingers in my ears. "You have betrayed the light. Sacrificing your divinity for what? A promise of power? If that wasn't crime enough, you coerced a Keeper who willingly sacrificed part of her soul to turn against her mandate to guide and keep souls from the darkness.

"You sold her to the primordial demon, who used her to target a multitude of innocents within the sphere of those she corrupted. How do you plead?"

Michael's words hit home. Lilith had corrupted Stan, but it was Arabella who steered them both to Charlotte. I had to tamp down on my anger, reminding myself that Stan was paying for his actions post-compulsion, and that Michael and Angelica would take care of their own culpable lot.

Zach scrambled to his knees and looked up at Michael who seemed to loom larger than life. The pain and regret in the former angel's face was pathetic. "Guilty." He bent to the ground with clasped hands. "I beg forgiveness and penance."

"Your fate will be determined by your willingness to purge yourself of everything you know and everything you did for the darkness. Who is pulling the strings, and what plans have yet to be executed."

Zach's head jerked up at that last word. I guess he was afraid of losing his existence permanently. Maybe Michael would take suggestions on how to punish this sorry excuse for an angel. Cade could show him his universe valve trick, and let him feel the pain he inflicted, even if it was on the periphery.

Zach spoke quickly, and his willingness to spill the beans of Lilith was impressive. He was the weakest link, and when he spoke of seducing Arabella on Lilith's command, I thought Angie would end him then and there.

One Scythe Fits All

Arabella was guilty of loneliness and being relegated to limbo alone for far too long. For that, the powers that be had to own their culpability in her fate. She'd be forgiven, but any possibility of paradise had been kissed away for the former Keeper.

Her soul had to be removed from my pendant before we made the next move. Angie didn't have to tell me. I already guessed. Arabella was too much of a risk.

When Michael had what he wanted, he snapped his fingers and Zach vanished.

"Is he dead?" Thea asked.

"No, my dear witch. He has been removed to a place where he will await his fate and no longer be a threat to anyone in this room or anywhere else."

Michael seemed satisfied with the plan that lay in front of him and Angelica, but neither said a word as of yet.

"So, what's the plan of attack?" I paced, ready for action. "Bix said Morana is in the ruler's lair, and the Keepers who were sacrificed would guide my steps. Should we uber to Penn Station or take the subway?"

"No, Louisa. This is not a task for you."

"Why not? Reapers are already wary of me. I'm not saying for me to go this alone, but I think together we make a pretty good team."

Michael sat in his chair again, templing his fingers against his chin. "You're right. Reapers are wary of you, but there is more to the darkness than just reapers. It's Hell, sweetheart. Literally. You cannot go into the darkness. Neither Angelica nor I could guarantee your safety. If Samael discovered you, we wouldn't be able to reclaim you."

"The same goes for Cade and Thea, as well. Humans cannot cross into that realm, let alone humans who are so very dear to me." Angelica was adamant.

I sat on the couch watching Thea gather her crystals. It was like déjà vu from early this afternoon, except we left the prison on a high.

"So, if Lou and I can't go, that leaves you and Michael to go into the darkness to free Morana and take Lilith to task." Cade sat beside me on the couch.

"We can't go either," Angie sat at her desk, rubbing her temples with the tips of her fingers. "We need a diversion that would lure Lilith to the surface. Something she absolutely can't resist.

My hand was on my pendant, and I knew it was time. "We have bait. In fact, we have a double scoop. Me and my pendant." I hummed the tune to "Me and My Shadow," dangling the mosaic in front of my chest like a pendulum.

"Are you crazy, Louisa!" Cade shifted on the couch to face me. He used my full name, so he was not playing. "This isn't a lowly reaper chittering from the shadows. We're talking Lilith, with Samael as the big bad doing his cheer from the sidelines and tripping us up at every turn."

I smoothed the pendant against my shirt, and then spread my hand toward Michael. "And we have Michael. Archangel and Sword of God. Not to mention my one thousand times great grandfather."

"Will you stop with that?" he shot back, shooting Angelica a dirty look.

"I'm not wrong, Michael. Not about the fact we have you in our corner. If we are all together, with me and this pendant front and center, neither Lilith nor Samael would be able to resist. If we lure them to the earthly plain, we level the playing field. We may even have home court advantage."

Cade raised an eyebrow. "No. Definitely no."

"What? I haven't even said my plan yet."

He snorted, shaking his head. "You don't have to. I know you, Lou. You mean our wedding."

I opened my mouth to argue the point, but then snapped my lips shut. Cade knew me too well, and besides, he was right.

"The wedding is the perfect ploy to settle all scores. Lilith will have to let Morana attend. There's no way she could pull off that kind of deception in front of so many people, especially when Michael gives the bride away.

"Samael won't be able to resist the chance to publicly thumb his nose at his archenemy. Especially if there's a prize or two at the end."

Angie nodded, and Michael actually cracked a smile.

"No." Cade stood. "It's too dangerous. Someone could end up dead or worse, relegated permanently to the darkness as Samael's puppet."

"Cade, please." Michael waved him back to his seat beside me. "I understand your apprehension, and I am with you on that one hundred percent. Except for one thing." He spread his hands. "Me. What if I guarantee that I will set right anything that goes wrong? What if I swore on my own divinity? The same light you saw peel away from Zachariel. What if I swore on that, and on my sword, that I would render any death incurred that day as invalid, thus returning that soul to life as they knew it? To ensure any injury, healed. Any damage, repaired."

The muscle in Cade's cheek worked overtime as he considered. "You'd swear to all that?"

Michael nodded.

"An indisputable contract, signed in golden angelic blood, between yourself and Louisa and I, for any and all of the above, for any and all of our guests, including Louisa and myself."

Michael was so still I thought his face would crack.

"Someone's been spending time in the archive," Angie said, sporting a proud smirk. "I told you I train my people well."

"So?" Cade prompted. "Angelica can summon Raguel. She can draw up the contract. Once we both read it and sign, it'll be go time."

Michael side-eyed Angie. "And how do your Keepers know Reggie?"

"You're not serious?" She laughed at the question. "You, Michael. You are the reason my Keepers had to enter limbo for an informal inquiry into the charges you and I both agree were bogus and trumped up by the darkness to throw us off the scent of their deeper crimes. YOU are the reason."

He blinked a couple of times, and then grumbled something I couldn't catch. "Fine. Summon Reggie and Enoch and let's get this over with. I have a one thousand times great granddaughter to walk down the aisle."

Chapter Twenty-one

"I'M NOT CUT OUT FOR THIS KIND of thing. Maybe a wedding coordinator would've been a better idea." Thea stood behind me at the vanity mirror in my bedroom. "I'm good at ordering flowers, doing the decorations, and making sure the wards are set since we're expecting the big bad and his demon, but I cannot do hair and makeup."

"You're fine, T. I'm not a glamour puss, and even if I was, my makeup looks terrific."

Thea mumbled something else through the bobby pins in her mouth, but I knew she had this down. In the end, she was as much a pit bull as me.

The brownstone had been a bustle of activity all afternoon, with delivery people in and out of the house complaining about the stairs to the rooftop. It got so bad at one point, I almost changed the venue to the back yard, but I had promised Bix, and a promise was a promise. Especially to a gargoyle.

Thank God for Angelica. After the caterer refused to bring the food up the stairs, she arranged for a temporary lift to be set in the narrow alley belonging to the brownstone.

Festivities were set to begin in less than an hour, so I needed to be done with bridal primping in case we needed one last strategy meeting. Neither Cade nor I believed in superstition, so it didn't matter if he saw me in my wedding gown before the ceremony.

October was dressed in full autumn finery, and Indian summer had graced us with soft weather. Everything was perfect so far. Except for the fact we had unwanted guests expected at some point. I had convinced everyone this was the right plan, but second thoughts had me chewing my lip and ruining my lipstick.

I looked at myself in the mirror, wishing Emmie was here with George. Seeing them in limbo was unexpected and wonderful, but it opened my grief afresh. I always missed Em, but today more than ever.

Cade had written the two into the contract Reggie drew up between us and Michael. He made the archangel agree we could visit them in limbo afterward, and maybe hold a small, second wedding ceremony for their benefit. I thought the vein in Michael's forehead would burst when he read all the terms.

I tucked a stray curl into my loose chignon style, dodging a swat from Thea's hand. "Don't touch. That updo is put together with bobby pins and hair glue. I even wove a spell into every twist so it wouldn't come loose until your wedding night.

Stifling a laugh, I pressed my lips together as if smoothing my lipstick. "The idea of a wedding night is pretty old fashioned, T. Especially when Cade and I have been sharing a bed for months. He just gave up his lease this week, so technically we don't even live together yet."

Thea pushed one last flower into the cluster around the chignon, and I turned my head both ways in the mirror. "Wow, T. My curls looks amazing."

She smiled, but then tapped my shoulders. "I'm glad you like it, but we're not done. I still need to get this dress tied up. Vintage is stunning, Louisa, but where did you find this stringed monster?"

"Actually, I didn't." I stood from the tufted vanity seat and moved to stand at the full-length mirror by my closet. "Angie found it."

Thea snorted, her tongue peeking out the corner of her mouth as she concentrated on pulling each individual corset string.

"I'm convinced this gown was something she had hidden away for hundreds of years. When she said medieval style, I'm pretty sure she meant *actual* medieval."

Thea finished, and I turned to look at myself in the cheval oval. Funny, really. I had covered this same mirror with a sheet nearly five months ago, trying not to see the shadows that followed me everywhere.

I didn't know then they were harbingers of a new life. A life as a metaphysical Keeper. A life with Cade. A life with new friends and challenges I never dreamed could be real, let alone lived.

The ivory hue of Angelica's gown looked wonderful against my skin. The silk dress was exquisite, with a square neckline cut low over the swell of my breasts. Boning fitted the bodice tight around my waist, and bell sleeves accented the full skirt as it fell to the floor.

A central panel flowed from my waist to the floor, embroidered with purple flowers twined with gold and white. "I've never seen a wedding dress trimmed in purple. It's beautiful. Does it signify something?"

Angelica answered Thea's question from the doorway, and we both turned. "Purple is a nod to Michael's lineage. I thought it apropos, considering your shared trace, and because he gave you and Cade everything you asked for in that contract. Assurances like that are very hard for angels."

Thea must've felt my shoulders tense because she didn't let me respond. Instead, she bundled me back to the small, round chair in front of my vanity mirror.

"Okay, bride, sit. I'm not risking my curves standing on that tiny, tufted chair to fit this to your head."

Thea motioned with the rose gold circlet Angie picked out to match the dress. She placed it on my head, making sure it was as secure as the chignon before letting me turn for the finished effect.

"You look beautiful, Louisa," Angie said, with her hand on her heart. "Stunning, sweetheart. Truly."

"It's all due to you, Angie. Otherwise, I would've been dressed in a white sundress and sneakers."

Thea cleared her throat and I laughed, lifting the hem of my dress to reveal white Keds underneath.

"You are definitely you, Louisa, even dressed as a medieval princess." Angelica checked her watch, and then looked at me again. "We need to get a move on. Everything is in place."

"Do we need to go over things one more time?"

She shook her head. "You and Cade are just bait. Michael and I will handle Lilith and anyone else the darkness spits up. I paid a visit to the Memento Mori roof before I headed downtown. Bix is already here, but I was informed in no uncertain terms he is here as a guest. Or as he put it, a guesssssst."

I grinned at Angie's gargoyle impression. "A small price to pay for the information he provided."

"Very true," she agreed. "Bix aside, the rest of his kind are under my auspices. I had them strategically placed around the rooftop perimeter. They know to give us fair warning if something wicked this way comes."

I inhaled, tamping down my underlying anxiety. "Gargoyles for the win."

"Again, very true."

Thea put her hands on my shoulders, ending our chatter. "Time waits for no one, not even a bride."

The two helped me hike my dress for the walk downstairs, and then outside to the temporary elevator.

One Scythe Fits All

I took my time, not wanting to break a sweat, swearing the next big purchase Cade and I made would be an actual indoor elevator.

We reached the roof with time to spare, scooting into the tented bride's room set to the side of the festivities. From there I had the chance to breathe and look around. Angelica kept me company while Thea checked anything last minute was put in its place.

"Any sign of Morana?" I took the glass of wine Angie poured for each of us. I didn't want to upset her, but the plan would be moot otherwise.

She scanned the crowd through the tent's opening, but from her face it was pretty clear Morana wasn't among our guests. Not that any of us expected her to waltz in dressed to the nines. It was more likely Lilith would show up in one form or another, with Morana in tow, but subdued.

"Have faith, Louisa. Lilith won't be able to resist humiliating my sister in front of me and Michael and everyone else."

The plan needed a backseat in my head for the time being. This was still my wedding, and I wanted a chance to drink it all in.

Thea had done wonders, with autumn wildflowers turning my rooftop garden into a bower. Mini spotlights added fire to the fall colors, while soft twinkle lights dotted the potted trees, their gentle glow adding an air of mystery to the twilight.

Cade stood with Jeremiah beside the floral arch at the end of the aisle. I had no idea he and the Manager of

Life Audits were so close. Then again, who did Cade have left from his previous life?

It was then it hit me what he meant when he said Keepers' lives can be a lonely existence. Everyone we know and love would pass on to their next wild ramble, but we would remain, along with Memento Mori. I realized then how lucky I was to have Cade beside me as we walked this very long life together.

Guests mingled, sharing the small cocktail hour before the main event. Everyone seemed to be having a good time. Thea chatted with the crew from the Jefferson Library, looking wildly vibrant and happy before rushing back to me in the tent.

Angelica blew me a kiss once Thea was back, and then left to take her place as officiant. It was time.

"You know, you should've let her be your maid of honor. She's dressed for it," Thea said, swishing the full skirt on her multi-colored halter dress. "I look like I belong in a caravan."

I grabbed her in a hug, not caring if it wrinkled my dress. "Angelica is always going to look runway ready, and you will always look like *you*, which is more beautiful than you know. Whether you know it or not, you're the sister I never had, and I'm blessed to have you in my life."

"Crap," she said, dabbing at her eyes. "If you wanted to ruin my mascara, Louisa..."

"Stop it. You know it's waterproof."

She laughed. "Like Angie says, very true."

One Scythe Fits All

The soothing melody of "Claire de Lune" began, cuing everyone to take their seats. The party was small, but everyone invited came, with most guests either from Memento Mori or the Jefferson Library.

Angelica stood at the head of the aisle beneath the floral arch, as Cade positioned himself to the right with Jeremiah at his side.

The music faded and the last note drifted into the twilight signaling everyone to stand.

"You look lovely, Louisa." Michael smiled, joining me at my side. "Are you ready?" he asked, offering me his elbow.

This was it.

The first strains of a soft violin floated down the aisle as Thea walked ahead of us. A rush of emotion took hold as reality hit, and I lifted my eyes to see Cade waiting for me.

I gripped Michael's arm, letting him set the pace so I didn't sprint ahead. I walked with my head high, with my pendant hanging in full view. It stayed cool against my skin, and I prayed it would stay that way long enough for us to get through the ceremony.

"Who gives this woman in marriage?" Angelica asked with a smile, eyeing Michael.

"I do," he replied, and the archangel had to wipe his eyes. The big softie.

Cade took my hand, and the expression of love and pride on his face filled me with such hope it nearly overwhelmed me. "You look gorgeous," he said with a wink. "Then again, you always do."

It never failed. Cade always gave me butterflies, and with the way he looked in his tuxedo, it was enough to make me lose my breath.

"You okay?" he asked, angling his head.

"More than okay."

Angelica lifted one hand, commanding everyone's attention. "Welcome all. We have gathered tonight to witness the joining of two lives. Of Cade Praestes and Louisa Anne Jericho. Two people of one heart and one soul.

"They stand before us, ready to declare their love and consent to be wed. If anyone can show just cause why these two should not be joined together, let them speak now or forever hold their peace."

I held my breath, wondering if this was the moment Lilith would swoop in and all hell would break loose on my roof, but there wasn't a sound. Not even a cough or a sniffle.

"Louisa and Cade," Angelica continued. "To pledge your love and respect, do so now by speaking your vows, and by the giving and receiving of rings."

Jeremiah and Thea each placed rings on the book in Angelica's hand. "These rings are a symbol of your love and commitment. A circle of gold with no beginning and no end, and so be it throughout your lives together."

Cade took the smaller ring from the book and held it at the tip of the third finger on my left hand. "Louisa, this I promise you, now and forever. With my heart, I pledge love. With my body, I pledge shelter. With my life, I pledge sacrifice. Forever our souls to keep."

One Scythe Fits All

He slid the delicate gold onto my finger, and Angelica nodded for me to do the same.

I took Cade's ring from the book and held it to his hand. "Cade, this I promise you, now and forever. With my heart, I pledge love. With my body, I pledge shelter. With my life, I pledge sacrifice. Forever our souls to keep."

Angelica covered our joined hands with hers. "From this day forward, you are joined in heart and in soul. Go forth in this life and the next as husband and wife."

Our guests cheered as Cade pulled me in for a kiss and then swung me around, making Angie, Jeremiah, and Thea all jump back.

"I think I married a crazy man!" I laughed, holding onto his neck.

"Crazy in love with you," he said, putting me down and stealing another kiss.

Hand in hand, we walked back down the aisle behind Thea and Jeremiah, and my heart was so full I thought it would burst. We were halfway to the receiving line when the gargoyles shrieked a warning.

Lilith was coming.

Thea and Jeremiah looked to Angelica who shouted for them to move guests to cover. An expletive left Cade's mouth, and he rushed me to safety as well.

"Stay here," he ordered.

"I will not! If you're going, then so am I."

"Lou, please."

"I'm your wife, Cade. Forget it."

Lilith swooped down in demon form, her black wings and taloned feet sending everyone screaming.

Morana struggled in her grasp, ripping free before tumbling toward the white runner at the edge of the floral arch.

"Never again, you demon bitch!" Morana scrambled to her feet, and the screech that came from her mouth was carnage incarnate. She whirled in full Grim form, her scythe in her grip.

My pendant was aflame at my chest. Icy hotness radiated through my chest and down my arms to my hands. This was different. No sweats. No inner inferno. Just energy crackling at the ready.

Lilith landed, her visage changing on the fly to mirror The Grim. One with seething black eyes, and the other glowing blue.

"This isn't one scythe fits all, Lilith! You've broken the balance and for what?" Morana circled, her body shimmering with flame.

"For power, stupid. For lust. For what should already be mine!"

Michael flanked Morana on one side while Angelica stood on the other. "Aw. Can't fight your own battles, little Rani? You need your big sister and her keeper to come to the rescue?" Lilith jeered, running one thumb over the edge of her glowing scythe.

A sound of moans and cries rippled through the air, and I knew my guess was right. Lilith had stolen souls trapped in her faux scythe. They could number in the hundreds if not more. We had to stop Morana from destroying it or we risked losing them forever.

"They don't really care, though. Or they wouldn't have left you to languish in darkness for months while I played your part. She laughed and the sound grated like chalk on a blackboard. "Your own sister didn't even notice when I was right under her nose."

One Scythe Fits All

Angelica's white light expanded, its brightness near blinding. It merged with Michael's, yet neither of them made a move. Why? Were they worried about retribution? Were they afraid Samael would declare war and shatter the contract between light and dark?

He tried that with Lucifer and Satanael and failed. Lilith was his bitch. If he wanted her to heel, she would.

My hands were aflame, and I crept through the empty chairs where my guests sat just moments before. Cade nodded. He'd give me the diversion I needed to get that scythe.

"Hey hell hound!" Cade taunted. "Where's your master? Does he know you're off your leash!"

Lilith whirled, setting her sights on Cade. With a hiss, she gripped her scythe, ready to swipe. "I'm not here to play with you, human, but I'll enjoy visiting you tonight." She ran her black tongue over her upper lip.

"Nice try, Lilith. You have no real powers. Not unless you count sucking poor sods dry while they sleep. What kind of demon has to invade dreams to get their rocks off?"

She hissed at him, her glowing eyes following his every move.

"What will Samael think when he learns you have to screw the paunchy and pathetic in order to steal souls?" Cade tsked. "The Ruler of Hell prides himself on being irresistible to all. He won't want sloppy seconds off cheap criminals."

"This is my fight, Keeper! Back off!" Morana growled, but Angie shut her up. She must've realized what Cade and I planned.

Hair triggered, Lilith kept one eye on the celestial three, and the other on Cade. She ignored everyone else, including me.

"See? Feisty." Cade went in for the kill. "Morana will make the perfect Queen of Hell!"

Lilith screeched, spreading her wings. I had less than a second before she shredded my husband.

"LILITH!" Michael's voice boomed, and the demon whirled. His sword sliced at her wing. The demon shrieked in pain but still took to the air, taking her scythe and all those souls with her.

"Louisa!"

Michael called my name, and his voice imbued me with his fire and strength. White hot ice filled my core, blazing through every sinew down to my Keeper's mark.

Cade screamed, and searing pain slashed at my chest, cutting off my breath. I wasn't hurt, but he was, and every ounce of his agony ripped through me. Angelica had joined our souls, and we truly were one.

Lilith's talons ripped through Cade's chest, tearing through his heart. I tasted blood, but it only lasered my focus. From the corner of my eye, I saw Angelica race to Cade's side. She enveloped him in warm light, and I could breathe again.

Lilith screeched, her wings beating the air. She lunged for me, her foul blood splattering the bridal bower. Instinct took over, power crackling through my very being.

The angel fire consumed me, glowing like a nuclear core. I was ablaze again. No conscious thought. No physical body. Just energy.

One Scythe Fits All

Lilith screamed, her body ravaged in the flames. I floated in the infinite, a ring of light crackling around me from head to toe.

I moved toward Cade, but my feet didn't touch the ground. Kneeling, I gathered him to me. Anguish so profound ripped from my rent soul. I screamed, opening my arms to blackness. He was gone.

Chapter Twenty-two

"I opened my eyes, wincing at the light streaming in from the windows. I had no idea how long I'd been asleep. Cocooned from the pain of my new reality.

Someone had pulled the curtains back. Didn't they know all I wanted to do was sleep? Didn't they realize I had lost the love of my life and had no interest in the hours, the days or the weeks that were ahead in an endless line?

I sat up, dangling my feet off the side of our bed. My bed, now. Scrubbing my face, I inhaled, finally taking in my surroundings.

"What the hell?"

Had someone come in and cleaned the bedroom while I was comatose after obliterating Lilith for killing

Cade? And where was my wedding gown? If Angelica had taken it thinking it would be kinder to remove it...

"Knock. Knock." Thea came in carrying a breakfast tray. "Rise and shine, bride. It's a beautiful day, and it's winding up to be an even better night."

I blinked at her. Had I lost my mind? Had she?

"Thea, what the hell are you talking about? I don't want any breakfast. I don't want anything or anyone. I just want to be left alone."

Angelica poked her head in the door. "Thea, do you think I could have a word with Louisa for a moment?"

"Sure." Thea put the breakfast tray on my dresser and then left, making a hoity toity face behind Angie's back.

She closed the door, and I eyed Angelica, shaking my head. "You've got nerve coming here today, lady. I know you're the Angel of Death and you have to do your job, but I'm going to tell you what you're going to do. You're going to get that bastard Michael, and you're going to hold him to his contract."

"I can't do that, Louisa."

I was on my feet at that, my hands clenched at my sides. "Cade had that contract signed in that archangel's blood! He has to honor it. If he doesn't I will take my pendant...that's right...MY PENDANT, and I will give it to Samael with my compliments."

Angelica just looked at me deadpan. "One of these days, you're inability to listen is going to cause you a lot of trouble. If you'd let me finish before going for my jugular, I would tell you I can't hold Michael to his contract because he already fulfilled it."

I blinked at her, reluctant to even breathe.

"What's all the yelling in here? Has my beautiful bride suddenly turned into a bridezilla?"

My knees buckled and I crumpled to the floor next to my bed. Cade stood in the doorway. Healthy and smiling. Not a mark on him.

"Hey now," he rushed to help me to my feet, sitting me down on the edge of the mattress. "I think you'd better eat something. I can't have you too weak to walk up that aisle later."

My breath came in short gasps, and Angie put her hand on my shoulder, calming me the same way she did at the preliminary inquest.

"Everything is as it should be, Louisa. You did it. YOU. You were the one who stopped Lilith. She's a demon, so she can't be destroyed completely, but she's incapacitated for millennia. Samael has been sanctioned, and every broken soul has been returned and healed. They are all on their way to their next adventure."

"Charlotte?"

"Charlotte, too."

Cade sat beside me on the bed. "Michael needs to practice his aim. He's gotten rusty since the last celestial war."

"Cut me some slack, son." Michael knocked on the bedroom door. "It has been epochs since then."

Angie's hand dropped from my shoulder, but I gathered it to mine. "I was so vile to you just now, and I'm sorry. Scion or not, I don't think I can do this anymore."

"I know," she nodded. "We let you down. You and Cade, both. It shouldn't have been up to you to save the day."

If Cade hadn't had the foresight to have Raguel draw up that contract, things would be very different right now. I wasn't willing to risk our lives and our happiness on something like this happening again.

"If today is really our wedding day, and everything except for Lilith and her machinations has been rewound, then I have a request. As a wedding gift to me and Cade, I would like us to be released from being Keepers. I would like to begin living our human lives from tomorrow on, but I don't want our memories wiped, and I don't want Cade aging one hundred and fifty years before my eyes."

Angie smirked at that. "We're way ahead of you, sweetheart." Michael pulled a folded document from his breast pocket and handed it to Cade.

"Those are your documents releasing you from being Keepers. It nullifies all prior penalties and allows for everything you asked for and then some. You will always be welcome at Memento Mori, and even remain in our employ if you so choose."

Angie lifted a hand. "As humans, in a consulting capacity. Like Thea. Of course, the door to my office is always open, and if you happen to change your mind, you both will be reinstated as level fives immediately. No questions asked."

Michael nodded. His face soft with a touch of melancholy. "You may not be a Keeper anymore, Louisa, but you are still my scion. You will always have access to my light, just not in a nuclear capacity anymore."

My hand went to my chest, but my pendant was no longer there, and I looked at Angelica for an answer.

"When I healed the other broken souls, I returned the pieces sacrificed for that mosaic as well. The Keepers who gave of themselves to create that pendant deserve peace. Emmie included. She and George have moved on, but they sent their love and blessings."

The Angel of Death put a hand in her pocket and pulled out the now defunct pendant. "You can keep this as a memento if you like."

I inhaled, closing my eyes with the pendant in my palm. Angie and Michael had given me everything I wanted. I had Cade. I had our life together. I still had Thea and everyone at Memento Mori, including Angelica. The moment was bittersweet, but the relief palpable. Would I always feel that way? Time was a great thickener, and if my days as a Keeper taught me anything, it's nothing is impossible.

My lids opened and my eyes sought Cade's. This was what I wanted, but what if he didn't agree?

"Cade…" I swallowed past the lump in my throat. "If this isn't what you want… if you want to remain a Keeper—"

One Scythe Fits All

"Lou."

I shook my head, so he'd let me finish. "It's your choice, and I will respect and support your decision no matter what. If we've proven anything, it's that nothing is going to keep us apart."

He reached for my hand that held the defunct pendant and kissed my bent fingers. "After nearly a century and a half, I'm ready for a break. We're in this together, love. For better or worse."

Angie leaned over at that point and pressed a kiss to my cheek. "Better eat and get some rest, kiddo. It's going to be a hell of a party tonight."

"Without the hell, I hope."

The angel snorted, and her hand flew to her nose at the undignified sound, but I still caught a corner of her stunned smirk.

"See you tonight." She blew me a kiss, and then she and Michael closed the door behind them, leaving Cade and I alone.

"Are you real? I'm not dreaming it, right?" My hands unbuttoned his shirt, checking for scars or wounds or something, but he was whole.

"I'm fine, Lou. We both are. Better than fine." He jiggled the release documents in his hand. "The only things that remain from our brush with Hell are bad memories, and those will be washed away when our wedding happens the way it should have in the first place. No one remembers what happened last night except you, me, Angelica, Michael, and Morana. Not even Thea or Jeremiah, or anyone else at Memento Mori for that matter. Michael thought it better that way."

"What happened with Morana? Is she still The Grim?"

He nodded. "With a much more improved outlook on how to do her job. She no longer answers to Samael. She now answers to Michael and Uriel, both."

"How is that possible? They both belong to the light. Won't that throw the balance off?"

He shrugged. "No longer our circus, so no longer our monkey." He snatched a strawberry from Thea's breakfast tray and held it to my mouth. "How about we eat, and then get a jump on our wedding night, Mrs. Praestes."

"Aren't you putting the cart before the horse by about seven hours?" I took the strawberry between my teeth, letting him take a bite so our lips nearly touched.

"Theoretically, we got married last night, but we can always wait if you want to be certain," he teased.

I pulled him down on the bed with me, and then scrambled to straddle his hips. "The only thing I'm certain about is how much I want you."

"Well then, Mrs. Praestes…" His hand snaked around my neck, pulling me into a kiss. "'til death do us part."

Have you joined my Newsletter List?

It's easy peasy lemon squeezy! Just click the link and boom! Done! Lots of book news and fun tidbits, and special email-subscriber-only specials! And don't forget to do an author solid, and leave a review, because every little bit helps!

https://www.subscribepage.com/mdambryemails

About the Author

Hi everyone! I'm Marianne Dambry. I write Paranormal Women's Fiction Romance. You might also know me as my spicier alter-ego, Marianne Morea, or even my young adult alter ego, M.A. Morea.

As you might know, I was born and raised in New York, and there's nothing like the city that never sleeps to inspire this writer's imagination.

I began my career after college as a budding journalist, and later earned a master's in fine art, from The School of Visual Arts in Manhattan, but it's my lifelong love affair with words and books that finally led me to do what I love most. Write.

I'm always interested in chatting with readers, so check out my Facebook page and tag me in a post. Or send me a direct message!

Books by my spicy alter ego, MARIANNE MOREA!

<u>The Cursed by Blood: Vampires</u>
Blood Legacy
Collateral Blood
Condemned
Of Blood and Magic

<u>The Cursed by Blood: Shifters</u>
Hunter's Blood
Twice Cursed
The Lion's Den
Power Play

<u>Club Vampire: The Red Veil Diaries</u>
Choose Me
Tempt Me
Tease Me
Taste Me
Bewitch Me

<u>Shifter Romance</u>
Torn Between Two Alphas
Her Captive Dragon
Taming Their Tailfins
The Siren's Mate
The Wolf's Secret Witch
The Wolf and the Rose
Never Cry Wolf
The Demon Hunter's Wolf

Whisper Falls Holiday
A Little Mistletoe and Magic

The Blessed
My Soul to Keep

CIA Rogue Operative
Dangerous Law

Like to binge read? **I've got SPECIAL EDITION BUNDLES** for an even better reading experience!

VAMPIRES
Special Edition Cursed by Blood UNDEAD Bundle
SHIFTERS
Special Edition Cursed by Blood SHIFTER Bundle
CLUB VAMPIRE
   Special Edition RED VEIL DIARIES Bundle

**Books by my Young Adult alter ego,
M.A. MOREA!**

The Legend Series
Hollow's End
Time Turner
Spook Rock

Made in the USA
Middletown, DE
27 July 2024